You Shouldn't Have

You Shouldn't Have

by

Susan Page Davis

And the peace of God, which transcends all understanding, will guard your hearts and your minds in Christ Jesus.
--Philippians 4:7

Chapter one

Light and movement coming from the back of the house across from hers caught Petra Wilson's attention. In the cool, May dusk, the lights in the family room of the big brick house flooded through the sliding glass doors. Inside, a woman gestured with one hand as she shouted and held a colorful object against her dark blouse.

Petra froze on her back deck, no longer aware of the rubber bone in her hand, or her golden retriever, Mason, waiting eagerly below for her to throw it. The woman's profile was framed by the patio door, and Petra couldn't see her neighbor's face clearly, but it must be the woman who lived there. Dull brown hair hid her face, but the slightly dumpy figure seemed right for—what was her name? Mrs. ... Hall? Howard?

"Starts with an H," Petra whispered to herself. The couple had moved into the roomy house last fall, and Petra had only seen the woman up close a few times. She knew almost nothing about them, but the homes on the next street were bigger, with generous lots and priced twice as high as those on Petra's street. Last month she had exchanged pleasantries over the fence about the balmy April weather with the woman. Of course, then there was that time Mason got loose and ran into their backyard. Petra preferred not to remember the husband's anger on that day.

A man stepped into her view inside the other house, and she recognized the tall, lank homeowner. She saw him more often than she did his wife, when he did yard work on weekends. He approached the woman and appeared to be reaching for the thing she clutched. They grappled over the object, and Petra caught her breath. The woman pushed the man away, but he came back at her. She slapped him this time, and he seized her.

The man grabbed her red scarf and pulled it tight. He was choking the woman. Petra gasped and squeezed the rubber bone.

Mason let out a little woof, but Petra couldn't look away from the riveting scene in the other house.

"Hush, Mason!" What should she do? She couldn't run over there, jump across the fence, and confront her neighbor. But she had to do something. Maybe she could scream or toss a rock toward the patio doors as a warning that his actions were observed. Then she would call the police. Her mouth went dry at the thought.

She started to move toward the steps, but suddenly it was over. The woman collapsed in a fluid heap on the carpet, and the man bent over her. When he straightened, he held the object they had fought over and walked to the shelves at the side of the room. Petra gaped as he lifted the thing and placed it on a shelf at eye level and then stood back. He turned toward the sprawled woman, then looked out the patio doors. Petra could tell the exact moment he spotted her. Even from the distance across both their backyards, the expression in his eyes chilled her.

She gulped and ducked below her deck railing, dropping the dog's toy. *Oh, no, what do I do now?*

Mason came over and stood at the bottom of the steps whining.

"Good dog," she whispered. "Just wait."

She looked between the boards that formed the railing. The man in the other house closed the drapes across the glass doors.

2

Petra took a deep, shaky breath and stood. Her legs wobbled as she dove toward her own double doors.

"Come, Mason!"

The dog bounded up the steps and glided past her into her living room. She closed the door and locked it, then hurried to the kitchen, grabbed her purse off the counter, and pulled out her cell phone. Her hands trembled. The last time she'd called the police, her world had gone to pieces. But she had to. She couldn't ignore what she'd just seen. Mason woofed softly and rubbed against her leg as she punched the buttons.

"What is your emergency?" a woman's calm voice asked in her ear.

"I—" Petra gulped for air. She looked over her shoulder, back toward the living room doorway. "I want to report a crime."

"What sort of crime?"

"I think …" She swallowed hard. "I think it was a murder."

In her dark living room, Petra couldn't stop shivering as she peered through the crack between her closed drapes. The crime she'd witnessed so close to her home terrified her. So did her thoughts of what lay ahead. She'd reported a criminal once before. The horror of that night twelve years ago still haunted her.

The family room in the house opposite was once more framed like a stage with lights aglow. She could see the actors. Two Portland policemen who had questioned her a few minutes ago now talked to the owner.

The tall man stepped over to the patio doors and gestured toward Petra's house, then stared out at her. She ducked back, then told herself that was silly. He couldn't see her behind her thick green drapes.

She ventured another glance. He was talking to the officers, and one of them appeared to be taking notes. The homeowner shook his head and gave an exaggerated shrug.

Petra exhaled and turned away from the draperies. No sense watching. If they found something, she would hear about it.

Mason snuffled her pant leg. She stroked his head, and he whined.

"Yeah, I know you're hungry. Come on, boy."

She turned toward the laundry room, and Mason pranced ahead of her in anticipation. Petra put a scoop of dog food into his dish on the floor. After filling his water dish, she pulled a can of coffee from a kitchen cupboard and worked mechanically, starting a fresh pot. Usually she microwaved one cup of instant at a time, but you never knew. The policemen might come back and accept a cup. Sitting down at the small oak dining table, she clasped her hands together and took a deep breath.

Lord, give me wisdom. Give me strength to get through this. Help me not to be afraid.

Tonight, fear had sent her back to prayer—an old habit she hadn't practiced in a long time. Not since she'd tried to do the right thing and someone she loved had died. Perhaps she'd been foolish to walk away from God; she didn't know, but maybe it was time to face the question. Later, though. Not now, not in the middle of this.

Coffee cascaded into the carafe. The smell of the rich brew filled the kitchen. As she rose to take her mug from the dishwasher, the doorbell rang. She hurried to the front door and peered through the peephole. One of the uniformed policemen stood on her steps. She threw the deadbolt and pulled the door toward her.

"Hello, Officer."

"Miss Wilson." His generic smile flashed. "We've talked to your neighbor, Mr. Harwood."

4

Harwood. That was it. Petra nodded. "Would you like to come in?"

As he entered the kitchen, Petra stepped back toward the counter to avoid feeling claustrophobic near the large man. Officer Stenwick, his nameplate read. His youthful features alternated between the meaningless smile and a grave, official business air.

"Would you like some coffee?" she asked.

"No, thank you. My partner is just finishing up with Mr. Harwood. We'll be heading out soon."

"Is there … anything you can tell me?"

He winced. "Well, cases like this are difficult, Miss Wilson. When the witness thinks she saw something—"

"I *did* see something." She noticed his pained expression and lowered her gaze. "I'm sorry. You were saying …"

"Well, we asked Mr. Harwood about his wife. He says she's visiting her sister in Millinocket, but is due home tomorrow. We'll check his statement, of course, but …" He pulled out his pocket notebook and glanced at it. "We didn't find any evidence of a crime over there."

"But … that's …" Petra stared at him. His impassive disbelief was clear. Just a lonely, single woman seeing things. That was how he interpreted this incident. "There was a woman," she insisted. "It may not have been his wife, but I saw her clearly. She was wearing a dark blouse and pants, and a red scarf. He used the scarf to strangle her."

Stenwick frowned. "A scarf in May?"

"Not a winter scarf. A decorative one. An accessory."

His lips twitched. "Well, I'm sorry, Miss Wilson, but we didn't find any bodies or red scarves over there. Mr. Harwood was very cooperative, and he let us search the house."

She swallowed hard. "He did?"

"Yes. Even the basement. We searched his car, the garage as well, and we didn't see anywhere that a body could be concealed."

"Then she's outside."

"We checked all around the house. Officer Chadbourne arrived on Harwood's doorstep only seven minutes after you called the dispatcher, Miss Wilson. There wasn't time for him to remove a body."

Petra's mind raced. "There has to be something!"

Stenwick shook his head. "We asked Mr. Harwood if he'd had company this evening, and he said he was alone since about two this afternoon."

"Then how does he explain what I saw?"

"He doesn't. Although there is a wide-screen TV in there. He wondered if perhaps…"

"Absolutely not! Look." She led him to the patio door. Her hand shook as she unlocked it. She took four steps across the deck to the railing. "I was right here. My dog was down below, and I was going to throw a toy for him." She nodded toward the rubber bone she'd let fall to the redwood decking. "You can see part of Mr. Harwood's television screen from here. But you certainly wouldn't mistake an image on the screen for someone choking someone else, would you?"

He exchanged places with her and stared toward the other house.

"I don't know what to tell you, ma'am. I'm sorry. But there's no physical evidence of what you claim you saw, and the professor—"

"Professor?"

"Yes, ma'am. He teaches at the university. He seems like an intelligent, respectable man."

Petra felt sick inside. "You will make sure his wife is all right?"

"Yes, we'll definitely check on her. Officer Chadbourne is calling Harwood's sister-in-law."

Petra licked her dry lips, not satisfied. "I mean … I heard them arguing once, when I was out weeding my flower bed."

"When was this?"

6

"A couple of weeks ago."

"What were they fighting over?"

She closed her eyes to focus. "The newspaper, I think. She was pretty loud, telling him to pick up the newspapers and things he'd left all over the room. They must have had a window open."

Stenwick nodded and jotted something in his notebook. "If we find anything, we'll be in touch, Miss Wilson."

The lights in Harwood's family room went off. Petra caught her breath at the sudden change.

"Please, Officer, I didn't imagine this."

He nodded. "All right. Can you just go over your description of her again for me? I'll check the missing persons reports for the next couple of days. If someone of her description is unaccounted for, we'll be back."

They went inside, and Petra sank onto the sofa with a sigh. She repeated everything she had told the two policemen earlier, concentrating on the woman's appearance.

"The thing she was holding," she said, sitting forward. "Did you look for that?"

"There were several knickknacks on the shelves," Stenwick said. "But you didn't say he hit her with it?"

"No. He just tried to get it from her. And after he … choked her … he took it and put it up on the shelf."

Stenwick nodded and stood up. "Well, as I said, there were several collectibles, and pictures of their grandchildren. But nothing seemed out of place or damaged."

"So … that's it?"

"Unless we find out his wife is missing."

"Or some other woman," Petra said.

"Well, yes." He turned toward the door and said a brisk, "Good night."

When he had left, Petra locked the door. Mason came and sniffed her hand, then whined.

Chapter two

"Come on, Linda, you can't leave." Joe Tarleton ran a hand through his hair as he scowled at his secretary. "I know you're having a bad day, but we can work this out."

Linda sighed and shook her head. "Joe, every day in this office is a bad day. I can't take it anymore." She plunked the contents of her desk drawer into a cardboard carton. Pens, sticky notes, envelopes, paper clips. Joe took them out as fast as she put them in, heaping them on the desktop.

"Quit that!" She slapped at his hand.

"I'm serious, Linda. I need you. What's it gonna take to make you stay?"

She barked a laugh and opened the next drawer. "I have two words for you."

Joe blinked at her. "Yeah?"

"Yeah. Health insurance."

Joe swallowed hard. "I can't give you insurance."

"Exactly." She picked up the box. "I'm starting tomorrow at the medical office."

"Aw, come on. Can't you change your mind?"

She slid her purse strap over her shoulder and headed out the door. Joe ran after her.

"That doctor's office can hire anyone. But you know the detective business. You're good with the clients."

"Health insurance, Joe."

She shifted the box and managed to open her car door.

"Please. Let's go get supper and talk it over. I'm buying."

She shook her head and shoved the box into the car, across the front seat. "You can't afford it. Face it. You can barely pay the rent. You should close this office and go to work for one of those big insurance companies you contract for."

"No way."

"That's your choice," she admitted, "but I've had enough."

The door to the storefront next to Joe's office opened, and two men in coveralls came out, each carrying two vinyl-covered stools.

"Hey," Joe said, "they're taking the fixtures out of the diner. Maybe somebody's remodeling it."

"Oh, they're remodeling, all right," Linda said, "but it won't be a diner anymore. Apparently it wasn't profitable. Sound familiar?"

"What's going in there, if not a new diner?"

She smiled as she got into the car. "A gift shop."

Joe swiveled his head to stare once more at the front of the shop that occupied the other half of his office building. "You're kidding, right?"

"No, I met the new tenants yesterday. They're very nice women."

"Women? You said *women*?"

"That's right. Goodbye, Joe."

A bleak sense of despair settled over his spirit. The workmen came out of the building again, this time lugging what Joe recognized as one of the booth seats. He'd eaten a lot of tasty cheeseburgers sitting in the back booth. Now he was going to have to walk two blocks to get a sandwich at the gourmet coffee shop or drive to one of the fast-food places that clustered out near the interstate.

"Great. Just great." He stomped back into his office. Linda was right. He was going broke. This town barely had enough desperate people to provide clients for the Tarleton Detective

12

Agency. But he'd toughed it out for fifteen years. He'd get another secretary.

It would be hard to find someone at the wages he could afford to pay. Linda was right about that, too. He needed a big case, or at this point, any case if it involved a wealthy client. Maybe he should run an ad, but that cost money, and ninety-five percent of his clients came to him through word of mouth. Either a past customer or a friend at the police department recommended him.

He sighed and looked at his watch. Almost five. He should drop by the police station. He might run into some cops getting off their shift and pick up some new leads from them.

As he headed for the door, his sleeve caught on a screw that had partly worked its way out of the handle on his top desk drawer. The button from his cuff rolled into the shadows under his secretary's desk. His *former* secretary's desk.

Joe looked at his flapping cuff for a moment and shook his head. Par for the course on this gloomy Thursday. He'd had a flat tire this morning, then Linda up and quit on him, the diner was being replaced by a froufrou gift shop, and now this. *All right, Lord. This is one of the lousiest days I've had in a long time. Are You trying to tell me something?* He didn't feel like waiting for an answer, so he went out, locking the door.

As he turned down the sidewalk, he almost bowled over two women standing outside the ex-diner. Both were looking up at the front of the building and didn't notice him until he pulled up short.

"Excuse me," he muttered.

"Oh, I'm so sorry," cried the nearest woman, jumping aside. "I didn't see you there."

"Sorry," her companion echoed with a bright smile.

Joe nodded. "No problem." They looked alike, and details like that caught Joe's attention. Not twins, but they had the same straight noses and creamy skin, though one was nearing forty, he guessed, and the other was several years younger.

13

Their rich brunette hair waved softly, though the older woman's had the slightest sprinkle of gray. Soft brown eyes surveyed him with frank curiosity, and he realized they must be wondering why he was staring.

"I'm sorry." He put on his most affable tone. "I'm guessing you're sisters."

The younger one smiled. "Yes, we are. I'm Keilah Wilson, and this is my big sis, Bethany Offenkuffler."

Keilah extended her hand, and Joe took it. "Hi. Joe Tarleton."

"Tarleton?" Keilah asked, her eyes widening.

"As in Tarleton Detective Agency?" asked Bethany.

"Well, yes." He'd have been surprised they'd heard of it if they weren't standing five yards from the door with his name on it.

"We're your new neighbors." Keilah grinned and gestured toward the future gift shop.

"Ah." It figured. If Joe hadn't been so preoccupied, he'd have guessed that. "So, when's the grand opening?"

"Memorial Day, we hope," Keilah said. "There's a lot of work to be done between now and then."

"We plan to carry a wonderful selection of gifts." Bethany smiled bigger than ever.

"So you can pop in any time you need to buy one," Keilah said.

"Terrific. And you ladies pop in any time you need a case solved."

They laughed and waved. Joe made his escape along the sidewalk, their cheery goodbyes echoing in his ears. Just what he needed. A couple of Pollyannas next door trying to sell him crystal unicorns and Maine shot glasses.

Petra woke to Mason's frantic barking. She blinked and rolled over to see the red glow of her bedside clock. 1:30 a.m. She sat up, her heart racing. What on earth had excited the dog? Mason usually slept peacefully on his cushion in the utility room.

She reached for the lamp, then stayed her hand. Instead, she climbed out of bed and tiptoed into the hallway barefooted, relying on the faint moonlight that shone through the windows to illuminate her path. She followed Mason's barking into the living room to find him batting occasionally at the drape that covered the patio door.

A shiver rocked her. The hair on her arms stood on end. "Hush," she whispered. He stopped barking and turned to face her, ears aquiver. Then he looked back to the door and whined. She stole to the side of the drapery and pushed it back with one finger, peering cautiously out onto the empty deck. She stood still, listening. Her throbbing pulse and shallow breath dulled any sounds from outside.

After half a minute, Mason whined again. She reached to pat him, staring into the night at the hulk that was Rex Harwood's house.

"It's nothing, Mason." But she knew it was something. He never barked at nothing. She let the drape resume its place. Maybe a raccoon had visited their deck. "Go lie down," she told him.

She went back to her bedroom but found she couldn't dismiss her fears. Every time her eyelids drooped, she stiffened and listened again . . . for what? She couldn't stop the images from coming to mind. The woman struggling as the man tightened the scarf around her neck. Harwood had told the police his wife wasn't due home until tomorrow. Was he sleeping tonight? Or was he coming to get her, too?

The clock now flashed four o'clock. She knew she would go to work with a headache. Not good. The emergency room nurses at Maine Medical Center needed to stay alert and sharp-witted on duty.

Petra breathed another semblance of a prayer and slowly forced her muscles to relax, concentrating hard from her neck and shoulders down the length of her body to her toes before finally drifting back into a fretful sleep.

Joe stayed out of the office as long as he could on Friday. The noise from next door was unbearable. Power drills, hammers, circular saws. Then there were the smells. Since the diner closed, the tempting smell of greasy onion rings ceased to waft beneath his door. Now it was paint fumes and cleaning solutions.

Last night, he broke down and bought a new desk phone and set up the voice mail account. He closed out a case he was working on for the insurance company and collected a check. It wasn't much, but enough to keep his rent check from bouncing.

One of the dispatchers at the police department had come through for him, and he had a new case. That was a relief, since his last missing persons file had come to a dead end. The client decided it wasn't worth continuing to pay him to try to run down her deadbeat ex-husband.

He missed Linda. Voice mail messages were a poor substitute. When he got to his desk late Friday morning, the flashing red light on the phone's base teased him with the promise of two messages. He cast about for something to scribble the phone numbers on and ended up writing them on the back of his electric bill. His first call was answered promptly, and he made an appointment to meet the potential client on Monday.

Wasn't there an appointment book somewhere? He strode to Linda's former desk and opened and closed one drawer after another. Back at his own desk, he discovered the book in his top drawer. He riffled through it, scrawled the woman's name on Monday's page, and told her how to find the office. Now, where was the second number? Oh, yeah, on the back of the electric bill.

Where was the electric bill?

He gave up and went to the coffeemaker. Linda always made the coffee. He picked up the can and shook it. Empty.

Too bad the diner closed, he thought again, as he went outside. The soon-to-be gift shop windows were sparkling clean now, highlighting the sad absence of a coffee machine or greasy breakfast sandwiches. Inside, he saw the two women opening cartons.

Bethany and ... what was the other name? Not that it mattered. He envied them right now. They had that innocent anticipation, confident that their new shop would be a raging success. He got into his car and pointed it toward Wal-Mart. They had a coffee shop there. He could get a decent cup of hot brew and some notepads before putting in some work on his case.

Half an hour later he drove back into his parking space, feeling better after two cups of coffee. He had just reached his desk when the door opened.

"Mr. Tarleton?"

It was one of the sisters from the shop next door. The younger one.

"Yes, ma'am," he said, rising. "Can I help you?"

She smiled as she advanced toward his desk. "Remember me? I'm Keilah. From the gift shop."

"I remember." Joe determined to file the name away somewhere in his brain, though he wasn't sure how to spell it. He watched her, trying to figure out why she was standing in his office. Just as she set a small wicker basket on the edge of the desk, a delicious smell hit his nostrils.

"I brought you some cookies. Bethany and I were saying last night how distracting it's probably been for you with all the noise from the remodeling, and we decided to bring you an apology gift."

"An apology gift?"

"Sure. We do gifts for all occasions."

17

He laughed. "Right. Thanks, but that wasn't necessary." The sparkle went out of her eyes, and he added quickly, "But very nice. Thank you."

Her smile returned, a bit strained now. "You're welcome. Chocolate chip."

"My favorite." He reached over and lifted the edge of the checked napkin. The fragrance increased, and he suddenly craved a bite. "They smell delicious. Would you join me?"

"Oh, no, thank you, they're all for you. But I did want to tell you we took a message for you."

"A message?"

"While you were out, a man came by. Bethany had stepped outside to get something from the car, and a pedestrian said your office was closed and asked if she knew when you'd be back." Keilah shrugged. "Bethany took his business card for you. He'd like you to call."

She held out the card, and Joe tried to suppress his eagerness as he recognized the name. Daniel Riker was a member of the city council. Things were looking up.

"Thank you, Miss Wilson." He pocketed the card.

"Keilah. We're neighbors now."

"Right."

"Oh, and there's one more thing."

Joe felt himself warming to his new neighbors. "Anything I can help with?"

"As a matter of fact, I was going to ask a small favor. Our new sign was just delivered, and there's only my sister and me and one man who's working on the shelving …"

Joe nodded, realizing he couldn't graciously decline now. "Lead me to it, Keilah."

Her smile was quite attractive. but he hoped this wouldn't become a habit.

He followed her out into the chilly May sunshine. Bethany and the handyman stood on the sidewalk looking at a signboard propped against the wall of their shop. The eight-foot sign was painted with a flowery, Victorian border in gold and pink. The name leaped out at him in large, fancy letters.

"'You Shouldn't Have,' huh?" Joe laughed.

Bethany looked toward them and smiled. "Hi, Joe. Yes, that's the name of our gift shop."

"Well," Joe said, rolling up his sleeves, "maybe I should hang a sign that says, *But since you did, maybe I can help you.*"

Two aspirin kept Petra's headache at bay for half her shift Friday morning, but she didn't feel as sharp as she ought to be. She tried to focus on her patients' needs. As long as she had to concentrate on a patient, she could forget about what she'd seen the night before.

But when she paused for a cup of coffee or sat down to do paperwork, the scene she'd witnessed from the deck replayed in her mind. She found herself shaking and trying to block the image of the woman whose eyes bulged as her lips parted in a soundless scream.

By mid-afternoon her hands wouldn't stay steady enough to hold a cup of coffee without spilling it. She went to a supply closet for a nebulizer required by an asthma patient, and when another nurse appeared unexpectedly in the doorway, Petra jumped, her pulse rocketing.

This is ridiculous. Too much caffeine. But she knew that wasn't it. Each time she regained her composure, the knowledge that a possible murderer walked free in her neighborhood came back to unsettle her. She still couldn't believe the authorities wouldn't listen to her, had just brushed her off as delusional.

Her supervisor approached her late in the afternoon.

"Can you stay an extra hour or so? One of the night nurses called in sick. I've lined up a sub, but she'll be late."

Petra groaned inwardly, but for the past month, since they'd been shorthanded, working extra hours seemed the only way to stay in the head nurse's good graces. She forced a smile.

"Sure. An extra hour won't kill me."

When at last she left work, the sky was blanketed in dark clouds and rain drizzled down. She walked out to the vast parking lot wishing she'd moved her car to a closer space when the shifts changed. Last week two women had their purses snatched in this parking lot. She kept her chin up and tried to walk confidently, looking alert. Thieves were more likely to target someone who seemed distracted or fearful, right?

As she reached her car, she noticed a man moving between the vehicles in the next row. His stealthy manner chilled her. She hit the remote opener for her car door and dove into the driver's seat.

With the doors safely locked, she looked around but couldn't spot the man. Should she call and report this to hospital security? It could be nothing. She drove grimly home in the rain, her back rigid and her hands clenching the steering wheel. At least she wasn't on call this weekend.

She got out in her garage and looked around carefully before closing the overhead door. Mason whined on the other side of the kitchen door.

"It's me, boy."

He barked and danced around her as she entered, and barked again when she shut the door.

Petra sighed. "I know I'm late, and you need to go out. Let me get out of my uniform."

Her cell phone rang as she slipped on her sneakers, and she pulled it out of her purse. The caller ID informed her that the number was blocked.

"Hello?" After a moment's silence she spoke again. "Hello? Is anyone there?"

She snapped the phone shut.

Maybe she wouldn't wait until tomorrow to drive to Waterville. She dreaded spending another long night here alone with Mason. Hauling in a shaky breath, she fumbled to bring up Bethany's phone number.

"Hey, Beth? It's me."

"Hi, Sis. Are you all set to come up here tomorrow?"

"No. Well, I was thinking maybe I'd hit the road tonight. What do you—"

"Terrific!" Bethany immediately launched into a muffled discussion, and Petra had to smile. Her big sister couldn't wait to tell Keilah. It was great feeling part of the family again. They'd lived out of state for years, and Petra had kept minimal contact with them. She'd isolated herself too long.

After a few moments, Bethany turned her attention back to the phone conversation. "Keilah says we'll hold supper for you."

"Oh, no, don't do that. I doubt I can get there before nine."

"We're still at the store working. There's so much to do before the opening, we've been putting in twelve-hour days. Come on! We'll have a snack and keep slaving away until you get here."

Mason whined, and Petra glanced at him. "Well, okay. I've got to walk the dog and pack a few things. I'll try to make it by 8:30."

"Great. No speeding tickets, though."

Petra chuckled, but her tight chest hurt. She couldn't help wondering about that anonymous phone call. How hard would it be for someone who wanted to harass her to find her cell phone number? Not all that difficult, she guessed. She listed it on her checks and gave it out freely to acquaintances. She went to the patio door. With one finger, she pushed back the edge of the left hand drape just far enough to give her a view of the Harwood house. Across the backyards, the house stared back at her. Its drapes were closed, too.

Chapter three

"Come on, Petra, take a break." Bethany came around the greeting card display rack with a smile. "Time for coffee."

"I'm almost finished. Be right there." Petra swiftly sorted the last handful of cards and inserted them into the rack's slots. All morning she'd helped her sisters clean the new store and unpack merchandise for the shop, but her mind flitted to other things.

Should I tell them?

She had come here for solace, but gleeful reunion had filled last night. Her sisters had delighted in showing off the store and the new house. Everyone was tired, and the moment hadn't seemed right. Now Saturday was flying past. She hadn't yet worked up the nerve to reveal to them her experience Thursday night.

When she entered the office, Bethany was pouring coffee for three. She'd set a basket of blueberry muffins and a few decorative paper napkins on the table. Her flushed face and satisfied smile told Petra that Bethany had found contentment. Her long-held dream of owning a business was materializing. Petra didn't want to spoil that. She hadn't seen Bethany so happy for at least three years. The sudden death of her husband had sat heavily on her sister. But now she was excited, almost carefree.

I shouldn't tell them.

Petra let out an anxious breath and sat down just as Keilah burst into the small room.

"Hey, look who I brought for coffee. Petra, this is the owner of the fine establishment next door, the Tarleton Detective Agency."

Bethany's eyes lit up. "Hello, Joe. Grab that chipped mug we were going to send back, Keilah, and rinse it out for Joe. What's up in the detective business?"

Petra looked up at the good-looking but slightly disheveled man in the doorway.

"You know how it is. I could tell you, but then I'd have to kill you."

His choice of words sent a shock along Petra's already sensitive nerves, but the handsome smile that followed his remark assured her he was just kidding. Keilah laughed and looked over her shoulder as she headed for the washroom with the mug.

Petra eased her chair over a few inches to make room for the detective.

"Hi." Joe's chocolate brown eyes settled on her.

Petra nodded and averted her gaze. Joe's keen expression and chiseled features were difficult to ignore. The fine lines at the corners of his eyes and the shadow of whiskers on his jaw didn't detract from his appeal.

Keilah emerged with the clean mug and poured a cup of coffee for him. "You needed a break when I looked in on you, Joe. Besides, I wanted you to come meet our sister."

His gaze skimmed over Petra again. "Pleased to meet you. I'm Joe Tarleton."

"Hello. I'm Petra."

"Petra?" He did a double take. "You ladies have interesting names."

Bethany chuckled. "They're names of places in the Holy Land. Our mother always wanted to go there."

He took a muffin and placed it on the napkin Keilah slid before him.

"Are there any more?"

"Any more muffins?" Bethany asked.

He laughed, and Petra made herself look away. His magnetic smile drew her as if she were scrap iron. Did Keilah have her eye on him? Keilah wasn't usually a flirt. But this guy . . . there was something about him. Even with the loosened knot of his necktie and the scuffed loafers, his presence had a definite effect on Petra. He looked like the downtrodden anti-hero out of a 1940s movie who would rise above his modest circumstances and save the world. Did either of her sisters feel it?

"I meant any more sisters." He stirred a spoonful of sugar into his coffee.

"Oh, sure. There's Sharon," said Bethany.

"Sharon is a place?" Joe's dark brows almost met above the bridge of his nose as he frowned at Bethany.

"It certainly is. And surely you've heard of New Sharon, Maine."

"Well, yeah. So, there's an Old Sharon, too?"

"Oh, great! Don't you ever let our sister Sharon hear you say that!" Keilah scowled at Joe, but her eyes twinkled.

Joe took a cautious sip from his mug. "Hey, this is terrific." He took a bite of the muffin.

Petra realized she was watching him—staring, really. She tore her gaze away and met Keilah's eyes. Her sister smiled and arched her brows in silent inquiry. Petra felt her cheeks flush, a common betrayal of her emotions, due to her pale skin and auburn hair. She sipped her black coffee while attempting to recover her poise.

"So, Petra, are you the baker in this group?" Joe asked.

"No, I'm just here to help them set up the gift shop."

"Petra is a nurse at Maine Medical Center," Keilah interjected.

Joe arched his dark eyebrows. "In Portland?"

Bethany said, "Yes, but we're trying to entice her to quit her job and come throw in her lot with us."

He nodded, still watching Petra closely. Joe's scrutiny made her fidgety. It was as if he was trying to read her mind. She lowered her lashes so she couldn't see his intent gaze—intelligent, piercing, inviting—and felt the tint in her cheeks deepen from delicate rose to what must be fire engine red.

Funny, his attention didn't annoy her. Usually when a man came on to her, she suspected insincerity and wanted to run the other way. But Joe Tarleton seemed genuine. He lacked the polish of the doctors and businessmen she met in Portland, but he had charm to spare.

"Joe is a detective," Keilah said, seemingly unaware of the tension between them.

"Yes, I think someone mentioned that." Petra nodded and bit her upper lip. The thought of blurting out her story mushroomed in her mind. She couldn't quite look him in the eye anymore. "Are you . . . with the police department?"

"Oh, no, I'm independent."

"He's a private eye." Bethany shivered. "It's comforting to have him next door."

Petra could think of better neighbors for a gift shop. Of course, she had noticed a boutique across the street. But still, a private investigator might be useful. She eyed him while he helped himself to another muffin and complimented her sisters on the attractive layout of the shop. Could Joe Tarleton possibly help her find out what exactly had happened at the Harwood house?

No, better forget about it. She'd already decided not to tell anyone else. The police didn't believe her story. Why should a private detective? And if she told her sisters and they dismissed her tale, she wouldn't be able to stand it.

The discussion ebbed and flowed around her, and several times Petra felt Joe's gaze on her. She hoped Keilah didn't notice. She didn't want to attract a man her sister favored. Maybe when she left tomorrow, Joe would focus his sights on Keilah.

Petra didn't consider herself to be prettier than her sisters, although some people seemed mesmerized by her vivid green eyes. Still, they hadn't helped her find the man she could spend her life with. *Almost doesn't count,* she told herself. *In horseshoes and hand grenades, sure, but not with Danny Carson.* She winced and buried that memory yet again. Keilah was the one Joe should be looking at. Keilah was so sweet and fun to be around, but she claimed she'd never been in love. She deserved some excitement in her life. A romance would be just the thing.

But as she glanced from Joe to her younger sister, Petra could see that Keilah wasn't thinking in that direction at all. After all, Keilah had purposely brought Joe to the shop while she was there, and had even declared she'd brought Joe to meet Petra.

Her sisters must have planned this, probably from the moment she'd called last night. They were trying to set her up with Joe Tarleton, the rumpled-but-attractive gumshoe next door.

Petra wasn't sure she minded, which in itself amazed her. She usually bridled at matchmaking attempts, not wanting to get into another complicated relationship. Still, it had been a long time since her engagement, which began with great promise but ended so badly. Another wave of heat surged across her cheeks. She pushed her chair back.

"Well, we'd better get back to work, or you won't be ready to open on Memorial Day."

Joe stood up. "Yeah, and I've got some phone calls to make."

"Hot case?" Bethany asked.

He met the question with another heart-stopping smile. "Well, lukewarm, anyway, thanks to that message you took for me yesterday. Thanks for the food. It was a pleasure."

His gaze met Petra's once more, his brown eyes assessing her. It was silly, but for the first time in ages, she felt a spark.

What would it be like to have someone like Joe to confide in? She wished she dared tell him about Thursday night. About Rex Harwood throttling that woman. About the awful moment when she'd slumped to the floor. About the terror that had chased Petra up here last evening, her hands shaking on the steering wheel. The bitter fear in her throat.

"Nice meeting you," Joe said.

Petra nodded, her outward calmness surprising her. "You, too."

They went back to work on the store, and Petra put her body on autopilot, opening cartons Keilah brought her and shelving the merchandise under Bethany's direction. By noon nearly half the shelves were filled.

"Let's eat out," Petra suggested. She took Mason out for a brief walk, then she and her sisters drove to a seafood restaurant.

Keilah sipped her sugar-free iced tea. "Petra, you really should quit your job and come up here to stay with us. Bethany and I rattle around in that huge house."

Petra smiled but shook her head. "Do you really think the gift shop will bring in enough to support the two of you, let alone three of us?"

Bethany sat forward, her eyes bright. "We did a lot of market research and income projections. We truly believe we're going to make it. And if we had you, everything would be perfect."

Petra reached across the small table and squeezed her hand. "Thanks. But I think it's a two-person operation."

"Don't you get lonely in Portland?" Keilah asked.

Petra nodded slowly. "Yeah, I do. I was thrilled when you two told me you were moving back to Maine. I hope we'll see a lot of each other, but—"

"But you don't want to give up your secure job." Keilah nodded. "We understand."

Bethany shook her head. "No, we don't. You could get on at MaineGeneral here in Waterville. I know you could. And you and Mason could live with us."

"That's tempting," Petra said. "I'll take it under advisement."

The waitress brought their fried clams, and they all sat back while she served them. Petra reached for her fork.

"Let's ask the blessing," Bethany said.

Petra quickly let go of the fork and bowed her head, hoping her sisters hadn't noticed. She hadn't prayed in a restaurant in years, or at home, either, until two days ago. She should have known Bethany and Keilah would never give up the habit.

Maybe it was a good thing she wasn't moving in with them. They would soon discover how completely she had abandoned her faith. It walked out the door with Danny Carson when she was twenty-three. Ever since then, she'd told herself she was looking for truth. When she found it, she would trust a man again. As Bethany's gentle prayer enveloped them, she wondered if she had been looking in all the wrong places.

For the remainder of the day, she put her energy into their work at the shop. Keilah and Bethany insisted they take Sunday morning off and attend the service at the church their parents had belonged to thirty years ago. For Petra, it was a futile exercise. She sat through the sermon without hearing a word. Her mind drifted back once more to the murder. It *was* a murder. Her brain would not budge on that.

But her distraction didn't seem to matter. Keilah's only comment as they left the church was, "I sure wish Mr. Hiland was still here."

"It's not the same," Bethany agreed. They got into the car and she took out her day planner and read off a list of merchandise that was yet to be delivered to the store.

"I want to hang those stained glass pieces this afternoon," Keilah said.

Bethany nodded. "Did you bring the roll of wire?"

Keilah winced. "I left it home. It's on the hall table, where I put it so I wouldn't forget."

"Why don't I go get it?" Petra asked. "I'll take Mason out, get the wire, and make some sandwiches for us to eat at the store."

Forty minutes later, Petra drove down the deserted main street. Sunday afternoon appeared to be dead time in Waterville, with all the businesses closed. She turned onto the side street and parked beside Bethany's car. She was surprised to see a black sedan parked nearby. Joe Tarleton, perhaps? Maybe he was in his office, doing paperwork.

She reached for the cooler that held the sandwiches and soft drinks, then drew back her hand. It couldn't hurt to ask his opinion. It couldn't be worse than what the policeman had said.

She glanced at the gift shop. Bethany and Keilah could wait another ten minutes. Her knees wobbled a little as she got out of the car, but she drew a deep breath and straightened her shoulders. Did you knock on a private detective's door, or was it like a doctor's office, where you walked in and announced yourself? Maybe he wasn't even here.

She tried the latch, and the door swung open.

"Well, hello." Joe smiled and rose from behind a sturdy maple desk at the far end of the room. "Welcome to my humble establishment."

Petra tried to smile back, but it was more of a crooked grin. She glanced around the bare office. Two desks, a couple of file cabinets, some extra chairs, and a coffee pot. That was about it. She faced him, determined to get this over with.

"Hi. I went home to pick up lunch for my sisters and me, and when I came back I saw your car and . . ."

Joe grinned. "Is this a lunch invitation?"

She swallowed hard and tried again. "Well, actually, no. That's not what I intended. I mean, you can join us if you like, but . . ."

He watched her now, one eyebrow slightly elevated, and his expression changed from pleased surprise to alert concern. She figured his detective expertise had told him that she had something serious to share.

"Actually I came to talk to you about business."

"Is everything all right?" he asked.

"No."

Joe rounded his desk and pulled another chair over from the wall.

"Tell me what this is about."

She sank onto the chair and took two slow breaths before meeting his gaze again. His deep brown eyes emanated sympathy, sweeping aside her doubts. She'd done the right thing in coming to him.

"I . . ." She laced her fingers together and held her hands rigid on her lap. "Something happened a few days ago, and I..."

Joe was silent for a moment, then leaned back in his chair. "Take your time. I'll help you in any way I can."

His soft, patient voice calmed her, and she straightened her shoulders. "I was doing okay with it, I thought, but then, when I went out to the house alone just now, I saw that someone had left a message on my cell phone while we were at church."

"Bad news?" he asked.

"No news. No anything. Just . . . a hang-up."

"Could have been a wrong number."

She bit her lip. She'd run through all the possibilities, but she didn't believe this was random.

"It wasn't just a missed call. The caller waited for the message tape to play a few seconds before he hung up. And the incoming number was blocked. I've gotten several of these calls since Friday. I think they're related to an incident that happened Thursday evening."

His eyes narrowed and he picked up a pen. "Tell me about it."

She looked up at him, feeling the hot lump in her throat that came with tears. This was not the time to go all weepy.

"It's okay. Whatever you tell me is confidential."

She nodded. "Thanks. Because I'm feeling the urge to bolt. I haven't told anyone about this. Not even my sisters. And the police think I'm bonkers."

He said nothing, but his mouth took on a hint of a frown.

Petra sighed. "I think I witnessed a murder."

"I see."

She watched him closely for his reaction. "Do you?" She leaned toward him, gripping the edge of the desk. "You don't think I was hallucinating?"

"I'd like to hear your story, but up until now, no, I wouldn't take you for the kind of woman who uses recreational drugs or sees flying saucers. And I'll be very disappointed if I find out I'm wrong about that."

"What do you have against aliens?"

Joe cracked a smile. "Let's hear it."

Petra settled back in the chair and told him as calmly as she could what she had seen through Rex Harwood's patio door. Her voice broke when she got to the part where the woman fell to the floor.

"She had to be dead. She had to be. Her face . . ." Petra shuddered. "I can't get it out of my mind. And if she were alive, the police would have found her in the house. They said he let them search the entire building. But he was alone. And they arrived only a few minutes after I called them."

Joe nodded slowly. "What do you think happened to the body?"

"I don't know! If I did, I'd have told them, and I wouldn't be going through this nightmare."

"What nightmare?"

Petra told him about her sleepless nights, Mason's uncharacteristic barking, and the anonymous phone calls. Joe made a few notes in a small notebook.

"Apparently this man is a professor," she told him, "which for some reason makes him more credible than me."

"Hmm." Joe rubbed his jaw. "And you've seen the wife since then?"

"No. The police officer said they'd check on her."

"I could look into this if you want me to."

It was what she'd wanted to hear, but Petra wasn't sure it would help. "What would you do?"

"I could look into Harwood's background, see if he has a criminal record, talk to some people, ask a few questions, like whether he has a quick temper. Ask the other neighbors if they saw anything that night. And I've got a buddy in the Portland P.D. He might be able to tell me if Mrs. Harwood has resurfaced. All I know about this case is what you've told me, but you seem to think the police did a crummy job of making sure no one died that night."

Petra's heart pounded. He wasn't brushing off her story, and she felt more confident than she had since it happened. "At the time, I felt as if they should have done more, but I'm not sure what. If your friend pokes around and doesn't find anything, it might just make Rex angrier with me than he is now, if that's possible."

"You may be right," Joe agreed. "I could do the background check, though. That wouldn't alert him."

She hesitated. Did she want to hire him? A private investigation would cost money. That wasn't a problem, really. She thought it would be worth spending some cash to get to the truth. But what if Joe somehow antagonized Harwood further?

"The police seemed to believe him. They took his story over mine. I'm not sure I want to upset him again. I mean, if he was outside my house the other night, and if he is making these phone calls . . . Can I think about it?"

"Sure." Joe reached into his shirt pocket, took out a business card, and slid it across the desk. "My office phone and my cell phone numbers are on here."

She slipped it into her pocket. "I'll call you in a day or two."

He nodded, and his lips curved upward slightly. "Now, how about that lunch?"

"Oh, right!" Petra looked at her watch. "Come on, they must be wondering where I am."

"You've got plenty?"

"Sure. Hey, let's not mention this in front of the girls, okay? I decided not to tell them about it."

"If that's the way you want it."

"Thanks. I don't want them to worry about me. And thanks for listening."

"Any time." He closed his notebook. "Petra, if anything else happens and you don't feel safe, call the police again. I know they've let you down, but they're still there to protect you."

She nodded, remembering her dismay when the officers treated her as though she were the wrongdoer. Joe's warm, brown eyes had the opposite effect. Things would get better. Maybe he could uncover the truth of what happened that night.

Petra couldn't help feeling anticipation as they went out to her car. Joe had just the hint of a dimple when he put his smile in high gear. Her stomach did that funny little flip she hadn't felt in years. She handed him the cooler and picked up the bag with Keilah's roll of fine wire. Maybe everything was going to be just fine.

Chapter four

That evening the sisters pressed Petra once again to consider moving to Waterville.

"You know you could get a job in five seconds," Keilah said. "And your house would sell right away. You're in a nice, quiet neighborhood, and there's a huge demand for housing in the Portland area. Please come."

"I'll think about it," Petra told her. "Now I'd better get my things and hit the road."

"Oh, can't you stay one more night?" Bethany asked.

In the end, the thought of entering her empty house in the silent night tipped the scales. Petra slept well for the first time all week. She got up early, loaded her suitcase and Mason into her car, and kissed her sisters goodbye. She drove out at 6:30, figuring she would make a quick stop at home to settle Mason, then dash to the hospital.

She'd been on the interstate highway an hour when her cell phone rang.

"Miss Wilson?"

"Yes?" She tried to place the voice.

"This is Officer Stenwick, with the Portland Police Department."

Her pulse picked up. "I remember you."

"I wanted to update you on the complaint that you made."

"Yes?" She pulled over and parked the car on the shoulder of the road.

"Our captain has decided to close this case. We found no evidence whatever of a crime."

"Oh."

"Yes, we interviewed Professor Harwood again, and also his wife. She's alive and well. They're sorry for the confusion you experienced, but they insist nothing happened, and the evidence supports them."

Petra let out a long sigh. "So, that's it?"

"That's it."

"Unless something new turns up?"

"Well . . . naturally."

Right. Her frustration nearly choked her, but she managed to say, "Thank you for letting me know."

The officer hung up, and she pounded the steering wheel with her fist. From the back seat came Mason's soft whine.

Suddenly she wished she weren't headed home to Portland. She wished she were staying at the beautiful Victorian house in Waterville with her sisters. She never, ever wanted to see Rex Harwood's face again. The offer to live with Keilah and Bethany sorely tempted her. If experienced nurses were as scarce here as they were in Portland, she could choose her place of employment. But it was a good thing she hadn't told her sisters about the murder. They would worry about her too much.

She pictured Joe Tarleton suddenly, with his deep brown eyes that radiated warmth and understanding. A man like Joe Tarleton wouldn't mothball a case after three days. He'd stay on it until he ferreted out the truth.

Joe looked like her best chance to find out what really happened in the Harwood home that night, perhaps her *only* chance. She gritted her teeth, knowing she couldn't let it go. She refused to live near a murderer and be silent. Still, finding the truth could be dangerous. If Rex decided to strike again, it would be way too late to call the cops.

On Tuesday morning, Joe meandered into the gift shop. He hadn't really expected to find Petra there, but even so, he felt a keen disappointment when he was greeted only by Keilah and Bethany. Keilah had donned coveralls and was holding a light bulb for a man standing on a stepladder. Bethany, dressed in a long denim skirt and checked blouse, was unpacking boxes of stationery.

"Morning, ladies." Joe held out a box from the doughnut shop on Upper Main Street. "Got coffee?"

"For you, anytime." Bethany smiled and took the box.

A few minutes later, Joe sat down with the sisters at the card table in the back room.

"Found a secretary yet?" Keilah asked.

"No, not yet." Joe picked out a butternut crumb doughnut. "And my voice mail account is bonkers. It told me I had three messages, then it erased them all. Or maybe I pushed delete instead of play, I don't know."

"You need a real person to take messages for you until you find a new secretary," Keilah said.

"Want the job?" He raised his eyebrows and grinned at her, and she laughed.

Bethany stirred powdered creamer into her coffee. "We're so busy I don't think we can take on one more thing. And when the shop opens Monday . . ."

"We couldn't go over to your office to answer the phone," Keilah agreed, "but maybe there's a way you could run an extension over here."

Joe sat still, thinking about it. "You know, I think the phone company lets you forward calls. I could have my desk phone ring in here if I didn't pick up after a few rings—if you don't think it would be too distracting. What do you say? It could save me from missing a job offer."

"Well . . ." Bethany threw a discouraging look toward her sister.

"I could pay you a couple of bucks per message," Joe said quickly.

Keilah pounced. "Oh, why not? It would help him." She shrugged at Bethany.

Her sister frowned. "Well . . ."

"He said he doesn't get many calls," Keilah said. "Can't be more than one or two an hour, can it Joe?"

He hated to admit it, but her estimate was optimistic. "Shouldn't be any more than that. I'd appreciate it."

"Oh, okay, but you get the phone set up. And if it interferes with our business, the deal is off." Bethany scowled at him, but she rose and refilled his coffee mug.

Keilah smiled. "Joe's going to have a new secretary within a week. I can feel it."

With the Wilson sisters taking messages for him, Joe felt that it might happen. He took a deep sip of coffee and asked as casually as he could, "So, Petra got back to Portland okay?"

Keilah's enthusiasm faded, and Bethany's face went slack as though both were greatly disappointed.

"Yes, she left yesterday morning. We tried our best to persuade her to come up here permanently." Bethany sighed.

"What did she say?"

"She admitted she's lonesome down there in the city, but I don't think she wants to leave her job. We'd love to have her up here."

"We'll tell her you asked about her," Keilah said.

Joe decided it was best not to ask too many questions. He'd learned through casual conversation that Bethany was widowed, but neither of the other sisters wore wedding rings, and there had been no talk about husbands or boyfriends. He'd wondered a dozen times over the last few days about Petra. She interested him, for sure, and he didn't want to assume things that might come back to kick him later. Still, Portland was quite a drive. If she wasn't going to move closer, there wasn't much point in thinking about dating her.

He couldn't help wondering how she was doing, though. If the story she'd told him was true, her lawn bordered that of a murderer. Her distress had shown plainly on Sunday. Still, she hadn't called. Maybe things had resolved themselves, and she'd learned that she'd been mistaken that night. But recalling her anguish and the clarity of her description made him doubt that. What she'd told him was true—at least, she believed it was.

"Okay, Joe." Keilah rose and gathered their coffee mugs. "You get that phone forwarding thing set up."

He made a mental note to send flowers to the gift shop on opening day. Or if he had a secretary by then, she could do it for him. Petra's sisters were about to have something to celebrate, even though they were unaware that their sister's life might be in danger.

Petra clipped the leash to Mason's collar and took him out through the garage. She was glad for the long days, with plenty of daylight left after she got home in the evening. Of course, tomorrow she had to work a double shift, and she wouldn't leave the hospital until eleven o'clock. When she and Mason returned from their walk, she'd have to call Alex, the boy who mowed her lawns. Alex walked Mason on days when she worked long hours. She locked the door and pocketed her keys, then headed down the sidewalk toward the park.

Eloise Burton, the elderly woman who lived kitty-corner from Petra, was just coming out of her gray-shingled Cape Cod with her Cairn terrier, Wexel, on a leash. Petra called to her and waved. Mason needed no urging to hurry his steps. They crossed the street and joined their neighbors near Mrs. Burton's flower beds. The two dogs woofed and snuffled each other in greeting.

"Your lilies are gorgeous," Petra said.

"Oh, thank you. I think they're extra large this year. The oriental ones out back are especially full and beautiful."

They ambled toward the park, and Petra was glad for the white-haired woman's company.

"Were you away last weekend?" Mrs. Burton asked. "I looked for you and Mason, but I didn't see you."

"Yes, I went to Waterville to visit my sisters."

"Oh, you have family up there?"

"Now I do. Two of my sisters bought a house together."

Mrs. Burton smiled. "How nice. I admit I was a little worried about you."

"Oh?" Petra paused on the sidewalk as Mason stopped to sniff an azalea bush.

Mrs. Burton leaned toward her and whispered, "I saw a police car in your driveway one night last week."

Petra had to smile. "Oh, that was . . . nothing really. I called them to check on something."

A frown deepened the wrinkles on Mrs. Burton's forehead. "Nothing serious, I hope?"

Petra hesitated. "You didn't see anything odd that night, did you? In the neighborhood, I mean." She knew asking was useless. Eloise couldn't see the Harwoods' house from her front windows.

"No. Not really. What night was it?"

"Thursday."

"Oh, yes. Wexel and I walked that way." Mrs. Burton nodded back behind them, indicating the way opposite her usual route toward the park. "I admit I was curious when I saw the squad car, so I walked past your house."

Petra patted her arm. "I'd do the same thing if I saw a police car in your driveway."

"Thank you, dear." They reached the park and set off at a leisurely pace around the perimeter. "The odd thing was, when I got to the far corner, the police car came out our street and turned onto the next one instead of going toward town. So Wexel and I walked down that way. We saw them stop at another house."

Petra opened her mouth and closed it again. The last thing she wanted to do was to frighten sweet Mrs. Burton.

Her companion smiled and shrugged. "I was mighty curious, I'll tell you, but I decided we'd best turn around. However, when we came home about twenty minutes later, lo and behold, the police were back at your house."

Petra nodded. "Yes, they . . . came back to assure me everything was all right. I thought I'd seen something at the house behind mine, and that perhaps someone was hurt. But it seems everything was fine over there."

Mrs. Burton's eyes glittered as she leaned toward Petra. "Ah, the Harwoods' house?"

Petra glanced at her sharply. "Well, yes."

"Thought so. That's where the police car had been. They're nice people, aren't they?"

"I . . . don't really know. I've spoken to them a few times."

Mrs. Burton nodded. "Once I heard him speak at the women's club. He told us all about the archaeological dig at Fort Williams. It was fascinating."

"Oh, is that what he teaches?" Petra asked.

"Mm-hmm, archaeology. And he's on the city planning board, too. Quite the star you have living behind you."

Petra's throat went dry. No wonder the police were so quick to believe him. He probably had a spotless reputation for brilliance and community service, too.

"I don't know him well," she said again. She hoped Eloise wouldn't ask her any more questions. Unless the police were ready to arrest Rex, there seemed no point in alarming her friend. Or maybe Eloise would take the policemen's side and assure her that the professor could never do such a thing.

Petra told her about the gift shop and how she planned to go up again the next weekend to help with the final touches before the grand opening on Monday. Memorial Day was the opening of the tourist season in Maine, and her sisters expected a good turnout for their festivities.

Thinking of going to Waterville reminded her of Joe Tarleton, and Petra quickly stifled the thought. If she recalled too vividly his sympathetic brown eyes and handsome face, she'd blush. Eloise would pick up on it and start asking questions.

She kept the conversation going until they returned to Eloise's driveway, managing to avoid romance and other sensitive topics.

Eloise paused and looked up at her before they parted. "I'll miss you while you're away. Wexel and I enjoy walking with you."

Her plaintive voice gave Petra a twinge of guilt. They had been casual friends for more than ten years, now and then enjoying a cup of tea together. Lately, Petra's work schedule had kept her busier than usual. She and Eliose hadn't spent much time together over the winter. Now that the weather was warm and the bulky layers of clothing were left at home, she realized her neighbor had lost weight. For the first time since she'd met her, Mrs. Burton seemed frail.

"Maybe we can have supper together one evening," Petra said.

Her friend's eyes lit up. "I could bake macaroni. Do you like macaroni and cheese?"

Petra laughed. "I love it. How about Thursday night?"

"Wonderful. Would you want to come to my house when you get home from work?"

"Sure. I hope they don't make me stay late, but I'll call you if that happens. Shall I bring Mason?"

"Of course."

Petra smiled and tugged on Mason's leash. "It's a date, then. I'll bring dessert and Lady Grey tea."

They said goodbye, and she and Mason went home. Petra felt more cheerful than she had in several days. She would get some apples and bake a pie. As she reached her driveway, she looked down the street. Her pleasure soured. Rex Harwood walked along the sidewalk, his black stare focused on her. Again, she saw his hands tightening the red scarf around the unknown woman's throat. The horror of the moment returned as swift as lightning. When she inhaled, she felt her own throat constrict, and she couldn't get enough air.

She hurried Mason toward the door and stuck her key in the slot. She glanced back toward the street. Harwood stopped at the end of her driveway. Petra froze with her hand on the key ring.

"Leave me alone," she gasped. Mason growled and tugged at the leash, leaning toward Harwood.

"No, *you* leave *me* alone." He glared at her then stalked across the end of her driveway, onto the sidewalk. He strode toward the park without looking back.

Petra hurried through the door, pulling Mason along. She fumbled with the dead bolt, then knelt on the kitchen floor and hugged the dog close to her, gasping.

Steady, Petra! He didn't do anything.

She made herself take deep, slow breaths.

Maybe he didn't do anything today, but he's a killer.

Should she call the police? She tried to think it through rationally. Mason whined, and she realized she was still squeezing him against her. She released him and stood.

If I call the police, they'll say it was nothing. And it was. Wasn't it? Except for her nauseating fear.

The next day crawled. Long before her double shift was over, Petra was exhausted. She called Alex's house to remind him to take Mason out for a walk and give him his supper. At first she'd hesitated to give Alex a key, but he was a nice boy. The arrangement had worked well for the past two years, since she'd acquired Mason. Alex's mother assured her that he had already left to head over to her house.

Shortly before seven, the supervisor alerted Petra to incoming patients. "We've got three victims being transported from a two-vehicle accident on the interstate. Make sure all the exam rooms are set up."

Petra and the other nurses rushed to prepare for the influx, and the frantic pace didn't slow again all evening. At half-past eleven, she dragged herself to the locker room and retrieved her jacket and purse. Her weary legs took her to the door and out into the fresh night air. She headed for the parking lot where she'd left her red Avalon that morning. The visitors' lots were nearly empty, but cars still crowded the employees' lots.

Her car sat faithfully where she'd left it, bathed in yellow light from the streetlight above. She was only a few yards away from it when movement off to her left caught her eye. Her hand molded to her key ring. Could she make it to her car safely, or should she turn back? She flicked a glance over her shoulder. She should have asked for a security guard to escort her out. Maybe someone else was going home, and she could call out to them. But no one else appeared to be leaving the hospital at the moment, and she hesitated. The moving shadow materialized closer than she'd expected—a tall man in dark clothing, with a baseball cap pulled low over his eyes. His path would intersect hers before she reached her car.

Petra turned and walked swiftly back toward the building. She thought she heard footsteps behind her. Many thoughts flashed through her mind: her cell phone was inside her purse, but she hadn't turned it on yet. Then there was the isolation of the employees' parking lot; the warnings the security chief had circulated; and mostly, how the darkness surrounded her. Was he really following her?

Unable to stop herself, she looked back. He was only a few paces behind her. A gleam of light flashed on something metal in his hand.

Chapter five

Petra broke into a run and tore across the pavement before the emergency entrance. The door opened and she slammed into a man just walking out.

He grunted and grasped her arms.

"I'm sorry," she gasped.

"Are you all right, Miss Wilson?"

She looked up into his face. Relief washed over her as she recognized the burly orthopedic surgeon.

"Doctor Bryant! Yes, but I think someone was following me."

She twisted to look behind her, and the doctor followed her gaze.

"I don't see anyone." He frowned and surveyed the huge parking areas.

"I turned back when I saw him near my car, and he chased me."

Dr. Bryant's eyebrows shot up. "You'd best get inside and call security. Would you like me to go with you?"

"No, thank you, I'll be fine."

Petra swallowed hard and entered the ER. She went straight to the nurses' station and made the call. The night shift supervisor came by while she waited for the guard to appear.

"What happened? Are you all right?"

"Yes. I had a little scare in the parking lot, though. Thought I'd better alert security and ask for an escort."

The supervisor nodded. "I'll tell the other nurses to be extra careful when they leave."

It was a mistake to tell hospital security about Rex Harwood, she could see that. The guard insisted on calling the city police. While they waited, Petra drank a cup of coffee and planned what to say. She hadn't mentioned to the hospital guard that she suspected her neighbor of murder, only that some unpleasantness had passed between them.

To her relief, an officer she'd never met responded.

"We've alerted our outdoor security to patrol the area where she saw the man," the guard said as he led the officer to the nurses' station.

"Miss Wilson?"

"Yes."

"I'm Officer Blake. I understand you had a scare in the parking lot a short time ago."

"Yes. I went out to my car to go home, and a man was loitering out there. He came toward me, so I turned and ran back here."

"That was wise."

"He had a knife."

"Oh?"

"I think so. There was something metallic in his hand that caught the light. They've had muggings here lately."

"Yes, I'm aware of that. Ordinarily we wouldn't get involved in something like this, where no contact was actually made. We'd let the security force handle it. But the guard here says you recognized the man?"

"I'm not positive. It was dark. He was wearing a hat that shadowed his face. But his build and the way he moved . . . As soon as I saw him, I thought of my neighbor. Now that I've. . .

calmed down—" She tried to smile. "That doesn't seem entirely logical."

Blake looked at the security guard. "We'll handle it from here and see that Miss Wilson gets home safely."

The guard nodded. "We've put one of our in-house men outside to help the outdoor guards patrol for the rest of this shift. Likely the man she saw is long gone, but we'll make sure everyone leaving tonight is safe."

He left them, and Blake pulled over a chair. "Miss Wilson, I'm aware that you filed a complaint against your neighbor, Rexford Harwood, a week ago."

She stared down at her hands. They were clasped so tightly that her nails were red.

He leaned toward her. "Ma'am, we've sent a patrolman to Mr. Harwood's house now to see if he was at home this evening when you encountered the man in the parking lot."

Petra's heart sank. "I'm not sure it was him tonight. I just ... it frightened me because of what happened last week. And yesterday he walked past my house and . . ."

"And what? Did he do something then?"

"Not really." She felt her lip tremble.

"Did he threaten you?"

"I . . ." She exhaled heavily. "Please, I'd like to go home. My dog will need to go out, and I'd just like to forget about this."

"Fine." Blake stood. "Let me walk out to your car with you, then I'll pull my patrol car up close, and I'll follow you to your house."

She stared up at him. "Is that necessary?"

"You think a particular person is targeting you. I thought you'd appreciate an escort home. I can check around your house if you'd like."

She felt suddenly foolish. Even if a mugger had planned to attack her, he wouldn't go to her house. And if by some wild chance Rex had waited for her in the parking lot, he certainly wouldn't hang around her house now that the police were alerted.

She almost refused the officer's escort. But if she did that, would they see it as confirmation that the man in the parking lot wasn't really Rex, and that the mental association she'd made was the result of an overactive imagination?

The officer walked beside her to her car without speaking. She drove home sitting bolt upright on the car seat, very aware of the squad car following a few yards behind.

Another police car sat in her driveway. At least the lights were off so the whole neighborhood wouldn't wake up to flashing blue strobes. She eased her car past it into the garage and waited until Blake and the second officer entered. As usual, Mason was barking on the other side of the kitchen door.

"My dog is very friendly."

Blake nodded.

Her hand trembled as she unlocked the door between the garage and the house.

The officers stepped into the kitchen behind her. Mason let out another bark and lunged forward.

"Down!" Petra grabbed Mason's collar before he could reach Blake, not that there was any danger. He'd probably jump up and try to give the man a kiss.

Her stomach twisted as she recognized the second officer—Stenwick, the one who'd responded the night she saw the murder. Just what she needed.

The big patrolman jerked his chin up and glared at the dog. Petra pointed silently at Mason, releasing his collar, and he slunk to his bed.

Her hand shook so badly that she was surprised Mason had obeyed. She sank into one of the oak chairs at the kitchen table.

"W-won't you sit down, Officers?"

"Thanks, there's no need," Stenwick said. "I just came to tell you that Mr. Harwood feels you are harassing him."

"That's . . . ludicrous."

"No, ma'am, it's not, from what he tells me. Now, I advised him that I would speak to you about keeping your distance and keeping your dog under control."

"My dog?" She stared at him. The tight, breathless feeling returned.

"Yes, ma'am. Mr. Harwood says your dog trespassed on his property about a month ago and did some minor damage. We have a report of the incident."

Petra jumped up. "Mason didn't damage anything! I asked Mr. Harwood at the time if there was anything I needed to have taken care of, and he said no, just keep Mason out of his yard. And I have!"

The officer shook his head, a resigned look in his eyes. "Well, Miss Wilson, all I know is that we have a record of his complaint against your dog, followed by an accusation you made last week, saying Mr. Harwood injured or killed a woman, for which our investigators found no evidence. Tonight you called in and said he attacked you in the parking lot at your workplace."

Petra gasped. "That is not what I said. And I did not call the police, either. The hospital guard did that."

Stenwick looked at Blake.

Blake cleared his throat and consulted his notebook. "That's correct. Miss Wilson reported a man chased her in the parking lot. The subject possibly had a weapon. And he was tall and built like her neighbor, but she couldn't see his face clearly. She couldn't make a positive identification."

Stenwick stood silent for a moment. "And no one else saw this man in the parking lot?"

Petra pushed herself to her feet.

"You think I'm making up things because Rex Harwood called the dog officer on me once?"

"No, ma'am, I'm not saying that. All I'm saying is, I advise you to stay away from the Harwoods, leave them alone, and keep your dog hitched."

51

His scolding tone was identical to the one her mother had used when she and her sister Sharon were caught thirty years ago using several of their father's silk neckties to hold the poles together on their teepee.

She bowed her head, unable to look at Stenwick any longer. Inside, her frustration grew.

"All right, then." The officer opened the door.

Blake hesitated. "Would you like me to look around the house, ma'am?"

"No, thank you. I'm sure my dog will alert me if anyone comes around here."

Stenwick eyed her once more, then gave a curt nod and headed for his cruiser.

"Good night, ma'am," said Blake.

Petra watched them from the doorway. They stopped for a moment between their cars and spoke in low tones. She reached up and savagely punched the button to close the garage door.

She turned back into the kitchen and locked the door, blinking back tears.

"What am I going to do?" she whispered.

Mason tiptoed from his bed to her side and nuzzled her hand. She stroked his head absently.

If they don't arrest Rex Harwood, he'll kill again someday. And I could be his next victim.

At the gift shop's Memorial Day grand opening, Joe entered the crowded store with caution. His eyes roved over the bustling scene. Keilah was at the cash register, and Bethany was helping customers. He spotted Petra at last, standing behind a white-swathed table that held a coffee urn, a punch bowl, a huge bouquet of yellow roses, and several platters of small pastries.

Joe's heart beat faster as he watched her. Petra was attractive in jeans and a polo shirt last week, when she'd come to unpack crates, but she was gorgeous today in a flowered sundress and sandals. Her auburn hair shimmered, and he caught the green spark of her eyes from across the room. Every move was graceful as she poured coffee and punch for the customers.

He edged gingerly between the displays toward the refreshment table. Why did women like stores full of breakable stuff, anyway? A woman pushing a stroller passed him in the aisle, and he turned sideways so his broad shoulders wouldn't brush the wind chimes or stained-glass mobiles. Even so, the chimes tinkled behind him. At the end of the aisle, empty floor space before Petra's table allowed him more elbow room, and he let out his pent-up breath.

"Hey! Good to see you." Petra's jade eyes sparkled, and she placed a steaming cup of coffee in his hand. "Sugar's right there."

He raised one eyebrow and smiled. She'd noticed how he took his coffee. That was a good sign. On the other hand, he noted a tense line at the corner of her mouth. "Things going all right?"

"Super for the gift shop. Not so good for me." She looked over at him with a crooked smile. Joe sensed he was a goner right then, though his past whispered, "Careful."

"Anything I can help with?"

She poured a cup of coffee for another customer. In a slack moment, she threw him a sidelong glance. "Remember what we talked about last week?"

"I sure do." He saw Bethany looking their way and smiled.

"I almost called you Wednesday night," Petra said.

"Why didn't you?"

"Because it was after midnight, and in the sober light of morning, I decided to wait until I could talk to you in person."

"Oh? New developments?"

"You might say that."

A customer approached, eyeing the punch, and Petra broke off with an "Excuse me" and flashed the smile that had brought him back here today. *All right, I'm dazzled.* But his sharp eyes also caught the little wrinkle in her forehead that spelled anxiety. He wished he could smooth that away for her.

Keilah approached him. "Joe, you've got a phone call."

"Oh, thanks." He placed his empty coffee cup on the table and nodded at Petra. "See you later."

He explained to the caller that he was in a noisy spot and took her number, promising to call right back, then hung up and headed for the front entrance. In his office, he grabbed his phone with one hand, loosening his tie with the other.

"This is Joe Tarleton. May I help you?"

"Yes, Mr. Tarleton. This is Belinda Stiles-Brackett."

He suppressed a groan. His divorce case. "Yes, ma'am. Did you decide whether you want to go on with the investigation, or have I given you enough data?" He slumped in his chair and put his feet on his desk, prepared to let her talk for five or ten minutes. In his honest opinion, if she had a psychologist to pour her heart out to once a week, she wouldn't be thinking of divorce. But she had turned up her nose at his suggestion of putting the money she was paying him toward counseling.

At last she wound down, and he reluctantly agreed to check out her attorney husband's movements on the coming Wednesday night, when he claimed he had a business meeting over dinner, after which he planned to attend the city council meeting. Sounded simple enough.

Joe hung up with a sigh. This type of case always brought back memories of his teenage years, when his father had walked out on the family. Maybe he'd chosen the wrong profession after all. Divorce cases were definitely not his favorite. But memories of his mother's situation always made him sympathize with the victim.

He wondered if he'd look too eager if he went back to the gift shop. Immediately, he discarded the idea. Petra was busy. It would be better to wait until she came to him. He didn't want to smother her. Still, he didn't want to hang around the office all morning. He'd head over to the police station and see who was on break.

The decision made, he jotted his itinerary for Wednesday evening in the appointment book and slid it into his desk drawer. Before he could rise, the door opened. His heart leaped then faltered.

Petra stepped inside, and the look on her face told him that he'd been right. Her pleasant attitude at the gift shop had been a mask covering her fear.

He jumped up and walked toward her, his hands extended. "Come sit down. Tell me what happened."

She pulled in a raspy breath and took the chair he offered. "Last Wednesday night a man was lurking in the parking lot at the hospital when I got off work. It was dark, but I thought . . ." She licked her lips, then met his gaze. "I thought it was Rex. I ran back inside and called security. And the guard called the police."

Joe sat down on the corner of his desk. "They called the P.D. because you saw someone hanging around the parking lot?"

She shook her head. Her eyes dulled with hopelessness. "I made the mistake of saying the man looked like my neighbor. The guard called it in and told the dispatcher. The patrolman who responded had looked at my statement from the week before."

"Oh, boy."

"It gets worse. I told the officer I wasn't sure, and when I thought about it, I realized it probably wasn't Rex. But it was too late. They'd already sent a patrolman to his house to make sure he was tucked in safe and sound."

"Sounds reasonable. They were doing all they could to protect you."

"Yes. Unfortunately, I'm now considered the girl who cried wolf." She brushed her hair back from her forehead. "Joe, the same officer who responded the night I saw the murder went to Harwood's house and got him up at midnight. He told Rex I said he'd stalked me in the parking lot, which wasn't what I'd said."

"And?" Joe watched her closely, taking in every gesture, every movement of her eyes. She looked directly at him. She was scared, but so far as he could tell, she was giving it to him straight.

"There was an incident a month or so ago. My dog, Mason, got loose and somehow wound up in Rex's yard. I'd barely spoken to the Harwoods before that, but they'd always been civil over the fence. But Rex got angry when Mason went over there, and he called the animal control officer. I apologized and offered to pay for any damage. He declined the offer. I could see that it wasn't anything serious. Since then I've kept a close eye on Mason."

Joe waited. This was leading somewhere.

She laughed without humor. "He told the cops Wednesday night that I was harassing him because he'd called the dog officer on me. The way he tells it, I made up this story of him strangling a woman to get even with him. But I wasn't mad at him when it happened. I was upset with myself for letting Mason get loose. I still don't know how he got over the fence, but he did. And now . . . oh, Joe, it probably wasn't him in the parking lot, but I've made this thing a hundred times worse by bringing up his name again."

Tears glistened in her eyes. Joe reached behind him and pulled a tissue from the box on his desk.

"Thanks." She swabbed her eyes and smiled ruefully. "All of which is a prelude to telling you I want to hire you."

He sat still for a moment, clicking through everything she had told him. Could he do anything to help her? If she had imagined the murder, digging into it would do nothing but worsen her relationship with her neighbors. But if it was real. . .

"Have you gotten any more anonymous phone calls?" he asked.

"Yes. Well, a few after I left here, but none since Wednesday. And he's madder now. That probably wasn't him making the calls, either."

"I wouldn't say that."

"You wouldn't?" She blinked and touched the tissue to her eyes again.

Joe got up and went to his chair behind the desk. He sat down and linked his hands behind the back of his neck. "Let's say he really did kill a woman ten days ago."

She nodded, eyeing him cautiously.

"Okay, so he bugs you a little. Calls your phone and hangs up. Why?"

"To annoy me?"

"Sure. To scare you and make you wonder if he knows what you're up to."

Her eyes widened. "You think he's keeping track of me?"

"Maybe. He's got to be feeling guilty, and he knows you're the only one who can accuse him."

"He walked past my house the other day," she said. "I was just coming in from walking Mason."

"Did he say anything?"

She inhaled deeply and looked away. "I was scared when I saw him. I . . . I told him to leave me alone. He said, 'No, *you* leave *me* alone.'"

"Did you tell the police that?"

"No. He may have, though. I felt as though he was . . . making a statement."

"A threat?"

"It wasn't that well defined."

57

"I agree." Joe sat forward. "Has anything else happened?"

"I don't think so."

"You said the police checked to make sure his wife was all right?" he asked.

"They say she is."

"You haven't seen her lately?"

"No."

"So you're not sure it's the same woman?"

Petra stared at him. "Well . . . yeah . . . I guess."

"I can check into it if you want."

"You don't think they did that when I told them her husband killed a woman?"

"I would hope they did. At least compared her to photos. Checking her fingerprints would be better."

"But they don't believe there was a murder," Petra reminded him.

"Right. So they probably didn't do that." He pursed his lips, thinking. "Well, let's say the man you saw in the parking lot at the hospital was Rex."

"The police said he was at home."

"Would he have had time to get home and crawl into bed?"

"Maybe." Her brow wrinkled as she thought about it. "It was at least half an hour before I got home afterward, and Officer Stenwick had talked to him, then went over to my house."

"All, right, so just for a minute, say it was him."

"But . . ." She pressed her lips together.

"What are you thinking?" Joe asked.

"It was the late shift. I usually get off earlier, but I had to work a double that night. He couldn't have known that."

"Couldn't? Or probably wouldn't?"

She watched him but didn't answer.

"How sure are you that it was him?" Joe asked.

58

"In the parking lot?" She shook her head. "Not sure at all. I mean, it looked like him, but I was so scared . . . and when I turned around and saw the knife in his hand, I didn't stop to try to get a better look at his face."

"Understandable."

"So you think it was random? There have been purse snatchings and muggings around there lately. Rex wouldn't be doing that."

"But a killer might use that as camouflage if he wanted to shut up someone who worked there."

She didn't move a muscle for a good ten seconds.

"Petra," he said softly, "I'm not trying to scare you, but I'm concerned about you. If you truly saw a murder, you're in danger. I can't discount that. You said you want to hire me. All right, I'll do what I can. And I'll start with the premise that you're telling me the truth and that what you say you saw really happened."

"Thank you." Her voice dropped to where he could barely hear her. "I'd like to have you look into it—you know, like we talked about. If you can do it without causing more trouble."

"I'm sure I can get some basic information. Whether I can find out what really happened that night, I don't know, but at least it will help us decide whether this guy is on the level."

"I just want to know the truth. I don't want to stir up things that shouldn't be stirred."

"I understand. And I want you to call me if anything else happens. If he leaves a message on your voice mail, not just a hang-up, I want to hear it. Or if he stares at you out the window, tell me. Any time something out of the ordinary happens, write it down. We'll document everything. Then, if he forces another confrontation, we'll have some evidence to take to the police."

"All . . . right."

He wished her voice held more confidence. "I meant it when I said to call the cops if you're frightened. Call me anytime, and I'll drive down there if you need me. But if you think there's the slightest chance you're in danger, you call the cops."

"I will, Joe."

"Good. Are you going home tonight?"

"Yes."

"When are you coming up to see your sisters again?"

"I'm supposed to attend a seminar Saturday morning at the university. But I'll probably come the following weekend."

"All right. We'll get together then. Meanwhile, if I learn anything pertinent, I'll call you. And don't hesitate to call me," he repeated.

"Shouldn't I . . . well, give you some money or something?"

"Yeah. Well . . ." He considered for a moment telling her they'd talk about it later, but immediately gave himself a mental kick. Since when did he not demand a retainer up front from the client? He opened the top left drawer, took out a rate schedule, and slid it across the desk. "Here are my usual rates. Why don't you just give me enough for a day's work and we'll see what I turn up. If you want me to keep going with this, we'll talk again."

She wrote him a check, and he reluctantly took it from her and pocketed it. It felt strange, taking money from a woman for whom he felt a growing attraction.

"Let me walk you over to the store," he said.

"It's only twelve steps. I counted."

He smiled, and at once he saw an answering light in her eyes.

"Come on. I'm walking that way anyhow."

He left her at the door to the gift shop and ambled on toward the police station, already planning how to approach Petra's case. One thing for certain: now that he was officially on the job, he would make sure she was safe.

Chapter six

Joe paced his office as he mulled over Petra's case. He couldn't stop thinking about it. If what she'd told him was accurate, she could be in serious danger. Even if she was wrong and there hadn't been a murder, her neighbor sounded like the type with a short fuse who might get violent if she so much as frowned at him over the back fence. And here he was ninety miles away, helpless to protect her.

He'd wandered into the gift shop once or twice since the opening, but Keilah and Bethany were so busy they'd only waved at him or absently told him to help himself to coffee out back. For some reason that depressed him, and he had gone to the grocery store for a large can of ground coffee so he could drink and brood alone.

He poured himself a fresh cup, stirred in the sugar, and carried the mug to his desk. He bumped his mouse and the screensaver disappeared, revealing his file on Rex Harwood. Born in Augusta, grew up in Kennebec County. Smart, earnest kid who served as a counselor at a camp for handicapped children, then joined the National Guard. Double degree in archaeology and anthropology. Taught at a private college in Indiana, then returned to Maine. Took a trip to Crete a decade ago to take part in an archaeological expedition. Summer digs at various spots in North America. He'd led another in Mali three years back, after which he wrote articles for glossy magazines on ancient history and the archaeological dig experience.

Joe lifted his mug and realized it was empty again. Might as well check into Harwood's teaching career at the two colleges. Maybe he could get an inkling of his financial situation.

An hour later he leaned back in his chair, eyeing his computer screen with a frown. It seemed likely that Harwood took a cut in pay to teach at the University of Southern Maine, but the school allowed him a flexible schedule for writing, speaking engagements, and professional travel. Probably a good trade-off for someone in Harwood's line. Not the most prestigious school in the country, but it enabled him to be a minor celebrity in his field and go off on Indiana Jones jaunts. He had a trip to Morocco scheduled for July and August.

Joe reached for the phone. A call to the academic dean's office at USM told him Professor Harwood was limiting his speaking engagements at present, but could be reached at his office on campus. Of course, the professor would be abroad on an archaeological expedition the latter part of the summer.

"Well, I'd like to hear him speak sometime," Joe said. "Up here in Waterville, we're always looking for something different, and I understand the professor used to live up this way. Kind of a hometown boy."

"I wouldn't know about that," the dean's secretary said. "However, his schedule fills quickly, since he's so busy, and if he becomes department head—"

"Oh, he's going to get a promotion?"

After a slight pause, the secretary said, "Professor Harwood is close to receiving his Ph.D., and he's very busy working on his dissertation. Let's just say his name is on the short list for head of the archaeology department."

"Contingent on the Ph.D.?" Joe asked.

"Are you . . . you're not a reporter, are you?"

62

"No, ma'am, just curious."

When Joe hung up, he reached for the phone again. Harwood had a lot to lose, and he was planning to leave the country in a few weeks on an extended trip. Time to call in the cavalry.

He had Portland detective Nick Wyatt's private number on speed dial. Joe couldn't see trying to keep too many numbers floating around in his head when he had more important things to think of.

"Hey, Nick, you got a minute?"

"Sure. What's up?"

Joe smiled. Even though they seldom saw each other and it had been fifteen years since they worked together, Nick was always ready to help him. Joe felt the same way. He'd canceled a date to go and help Nick once, and his girlfriend had broken up with him because of it. Well, not *just* because of that, but she'd fussed and fumed and told him it was the last straw. She'd planned a dinner with her parents for weeks, and she'd changed the date twice because he'd taken on a time-consuming surveillance case. Then Nick called with an urgent request. He knew Nick would not say "urgent" if it weren't life or death. But some women didn't understand a relationship like that between guys. Joe had called a moratorium on dating since that episode.

"I wondered if you could do me a small favor," he said to Nick.

"If it's legal."

"Yeah, sure. Could you pull up the police report on a complaint filed a couple of weeks ago by a Miss Petra Wilson of Acton Street?"

"Is this a case you're working on?"

"Yeah. She's my client."

"Well, I'll have to get back to you later, when I have a chance to check the computer."

"Sure. Call me anytime at my office or on my cell."

"What sort of complaint is it?"

"She claims a fellow named Harwood strangled a woman, and she saw it. But the investigators didn't find anything."

"Huh. That's an odd one."

"I thought the same thing. And I've checked this guy's background with my limited resources. No police record that I could find. He's a professor at USM, and he's a member of the Portland planning board. He seems squeaky clean, but still . . ."

"Okay, I'll see what I can do."

Joe felt a little better. Nick understood him. He would make this a priority. When it came down to it, Nick knew him better than anyone else on earth. They were together during the shooting that had influenced Joe to leave the police force and start his own private detective agency.

He decided to give Petra's case a rest and call the two women whose numbers Bethany and Keilah had taken in response to his classified ad for a secretary. The first one had already found a job, but the second sounded like a possibility. He set up an interview with her for the next day, then threw a few files in his briefcase. Time to go home and change clothes and then go park himself near the home of Bill Watson, a man he was watching for the insurance company that subcontracted him. Watson claimed he was in too much pain to go to work and couldn't stand up for more than ten minutes, but Joe had learned he and his wife were on the guest list for a charity dinner and auction that evening. Joe had finagled a ticket. He would follow the Watsons to the hall where the event was being held and keep an eagle eye on the subject.

Two hours later, Joe used his cell phone to click a fourth photo of Bill Watson circling the silent auction tables with a glass in his hand and peering at the merchandise. Watson had been on his feet for more than forty minutes and didn't seem to be limping.

His phone chimed softly, and Joe headed for the entry as he took the call.

"Yeah, Nick?"

"Okay, I've got the file open. Bob Stenwick and Eric Chadbourne responded the night Ms. Wilson claimed she witnessed a murder."

"Detectives?"

"No, patrolmen. They talked to Ms. Wilson, then went to the house where she said she saw the assault. Apparently she witnessed it—or claimed she did—from her backyard. But the officers found zilch. They decided Ms. Wilson was very suggestible and imagined she saw something."

Joe groaned. "See, ordinarily I'd take that at face value. Only I know her, and she's not like that."

"What can I tell ya?"

"Well, do you see another call she made a few days later, saying a man followed her in the parking lot where she works?"

"Uh . . . yeah, here it is," Nick said. "She claims he may have had a knife, and he sort of looked like Harwood. Not much there."

"No, but the police visited Harwood again because of it, and that riled him up. She's scared of him, big time."

"Yeah?" Nick paused. "Well, the report makes reference to an earlier complaint Harwood made against her. Loose dog. He called the animal control officer. Stenwick seemed to think the lady was carrying a grudge for that."

"Naw." Joe leaned against the wall in the entryway. "I know all about that, and I don't buy it. This gal is sharp, but not at all vengeful."

"I don't know, Joe. She's made a serious accusation against him, and he must be worried she'll ruin his reputation."

"Yeah, well, I'll take that under advisement. He does have quite a reputation to maintain. But about this alleged murder, no Jane Does have turned up down there in the last two weeks, have they?"

"Uh-uh. I'd know about that."

"Any chance you could take a look at the missus? She was away when this thing supposedly happened, and now she's back. I'd just like to know for sure he didn't do in his wife and get someone else to pose as her for the patrolmen on the case. Of course, you'd have to do it without the Harwoods knowing about it. If he finds out someone is still looking at him, he'll probably get upset again."

"You don't ask much, do you?"

Joe smiled. "Maybe I'd better drive down there and take a look at her myself."

"No, no. I can get her driver's license picture and see if she matches that. But I can't ask anyone to run fingerprints or get a DNA sample or anything like that for you, Joe."

"I know. Thanks, Nick."

Joe snapped his phone shut and headed for the parking lot. He had enough photos of Watson, and he didn't really feel like eating rubber chicken.

The next day was a busy one, what with his report to the insurance agency, interviewing the wannabe secretary—who, it turned out, refused to work on a PC instead of her adored Macs—and tracking down a deadbeat dad who owed three years in back child support. Work was picking up, and he hardly had time to think about Petra's case, except when he stopped at Burger King for a sandwich and onion rings. *Not as good as the old diner's.*

As he ate, he found himself ruminating on her lovely face, poignant with anxiety as she faced him across his desk and said, "I think I witnessed a murder." He'd about given up on complex relationships since that debacle with Angela over the meet-the-parents dinner. That had finalized it for him. That and the memory of his own parents' rocky relationship.

But Petra was different. She didn't seem the type who would pout when a man had to work late on an important case or drive to Portland unexpectedly to help a friend. Petra seemed genuinely interested in him, but was it just because he was a

66

detective and she had a problem? He didn't think so. That sparkle in her eyes when he entered the gift shop on Monday. . .

He'd about used up the time she'd paid for, and for what? To learn that Rex Harwood was perhaps the last man he would suspect of murder, let alone mugging women in parking lots? That bothered him a lot. Of course, Petra had decided that one wasn't really Rex. Joe wasn't so sure. A man who knew the nurse living behind the back fence could ruin him might take desperate measures. Maybe it was time he took a ride to Portland. He could hang around the university and talk to some of Harwood's colleagues and students.

The murder Petra described sounded like a spur-of-the-moment thing, not premeditated. A man who killed that way must have a short fuse. He wondered if Harwood had ever lost his temper in the classroom. He couldn't be too volatile, or the administration wouldn't value him so highly. But it was worth looking into.

Nick's next call came late in the afternoon, as Joe was downloading Harwood's speaking schedule from the college website, in hopes of catching one of his lectures.

"Okay, pal, you owe me big time," Nick said when he answered.

"What? You've got something?" The back of Joe's neck tingled.

"Just four hours of my time. I couldn't quit thinking about your oddball case, and today I took my life in my hands and asked the detective sergeant to take a peek at it. He thinks the patrolmen went by the book and nothing will come of it, but he agreed to let me put in half a day on it. I'll be in court tomorrow morning, but I thought I'd spend the afternoon in Harwood's neighborhood. Maybe I can take a look at the scene of the alleged crime and talk to some of the neighbors, see if Stenwick and Chadbourne missed anything."

"Let me come with you."

"Joe, no. I'm hoping for a promotion when the sergeant retires. If I mess up on this, I can kiss that opportunity goodbye."

"Hey, I'll keep my mouth shut. You can do all the talking. Come on, Nicky, you know I can be discreet."

Nick groaned. "I shouldn't have told you until I'd already done it."

"Please?" Joe decided he'd better play his ace. "Red Sox tickets."

"You're bluffing."

"Am not. June twenty-fourth, right on the third base line. I solved a case for a hotshot realtor who's a city councilor up here, and that was my bonus."

"How many tickets?"

"Four."

"Good night! What did you do for him?"

"Brought his teen-aged daughter home safe and sound."

"Well. You, me, Robyn and who?"

"What, you'll take your wife and let me keep two tickets?"

"Only if you bring a date. Old cop buddies and relatives don't count."

"I can handle it. Where do I meet you tomorrow?"

Nick sighed. "That vacant gas station on Congress Street, at one."

"I'll be there." Joe hung up and checked his schedule for the next day. Nothing he couldn't shuffle. Clinching the date for the Sox game would be harder. Of course, Petra was the only woman he wanted to take. Would she accept a date with him? Did she even like baseball? There was so much he didn't know about her. He turned back to the computer, determined to solve her case.

Petra tossed the rubber bone listlessly across the grass. Mason fetched it and bounced back to her, panting and begging with his eyes for a stroll to the park. She had curtailed their walking itinerary lately.

It wasn't just that her long hours at work brought her home exhausted. The memory of Rex Harwood's violence affected her more than she liked to admit. She startled easily now and hated walking in the open, where she felt exposed and vulnerable, even with her dog along. Mason would have to be satisfied with the romp he'd had with Wexel at Mrs. Burton's last night and her evening playtimes with him in the backyard. Next weekend, when they went up to Waterville, she could take him on some long rambles. But first she had to get through this weekend. On Saturday, she had to attend the seminar on breakthroughs in hematology at the university. Just the thought of going onto the campus where Rex Harwood taught made her nervous, though she knew it was unlikely he'd be there on a Saturday after the spring semester had ended.

She wrestled with Mason for a few seconds, until he let her take the toy from his teeth. She tossed it again, to the far corner of the yard.

At the sound of a door sliding on its metal tracks, she stiffened and turned her back to the Harwoods' property. She wouldn't speak to either of the Harwoods or even look their way.

"Come on, boy!" She headed for her back deck. *It's not right. I should be able to use my own yard without being intimidated.*

Mason pranced to her side, eager for another tussle over the toy, but Petra's heart wasn't in it. What did the police expect her to do? Build a ten-foot fence so she couldn't see into the Harwoods' family room from the height of her deck?

"Hey!"

She couldn't ignore his sharp call. With her foot on the bottom step, she turned. Harwood glared at her over the cedar fence. She considered going into the house without replying. But why should she? She had every right to be out here. Maybe she would tell him that and bring out a lawn chair and a book and park herself on the deck for an hour, until the daylight faded.

Maybe.

"Good evening." She raised her chin just a tad. No matter what she decided to do next, she wouldn't let him see that he'd scared her.

"You know I've done nothing to you."

She scrunched up her eyes, thinking about that for a split second. "I see no reason to talk to you. Come on, Mason." She mounted the steps, and Mason bounded up them and waited expectantly by the door.

"You're ruining my life," Harwood shouted.

Petra filled her lungs with air. Probably best not to answer that. But something in her, something that demanded truth, made her pivot and stare at him again.

"Look, you know what you did, and I know what I saw. Right now the police accept your version. Until that changes, we have nothing to discuss."

She took the final two steps to open the door. Her heart raced as though she had run a sprint.

After locking the door and pulling the drapes, she flopped onto the couch. Sweat beaded on her forehead, and an awful, empty feeling clenched her stomach. Mason sidled up to her and licked her hand. She stroked his head absently. Was this what she had to look forward to? Isolation and condemnation?

"Dear God, please help me." She sobbed and rubbed her eyes. She was so tired! The stressful environment at work since several nurses had left the department was getting to everyone, and she had to concentrate not to let her patients see that. Once more she considered changing jobs and moving to Waterville. Why not? There was nothing to keep her here.

And she'd be closer to Joe.

She lay back on the cushions. Did she want to think about this now? Her attraction to Joe was growing, no question. For

70

the first time since Danny, she had serious thoughts of getting involved with a man. Falling in love was so risky. Was it worth it? She knew the pain that could follow if you fell for the man you thought you knew, and later you discovered his true nature wasn't what you'd envisioned. But there were good, long-lasting marriages. She'd seen a few.

Something inside her whispered, *You may have grown up, but you're still not ready.*

Why not? she asked herself again.

Because you can't share your life with someone unless you have the same goals and convictions. You have to start on the same page. But you don't even know what you believe.

It was true. She'd left her innocent faith behind when Danny brought evil into her life and left it a smoking ruin. Everything had seemed so wonderful at first, and she'd overlooked the little things that bothered her. His odd assortment of friends, his erratic moods. After she'd accepted his engagement ring, things had taken a downturn. He lost his job, but seemed apathetic about looking for a new one. He came up with spurts of cash that he claimed came from occasional jobs as a construction site helper. Petra had suspicions, but she gave him the benefit of a doubt. Then she found the drugs in his truck.

The confrontation that followed shredded her heart. She'd hoped he would deny everything and have a reasonable explanation. Instead, he'd lashed out at her. She'd kept the information she had to herself for several miserable days. Then she learned he was heading for a transaction that would put a huge amount of cocaine on the streets of Waterville. She didn't know what to do. She couldn't turn to her family with this horrible knowledge. Finally, she did what she felt was the only thing she could do. She called the police, and when they went after him, Danny led them on a desperate chase that ended in his death.

Her family had offered their loving sympathy, but they couldn't know how deeply she'd been shaken. Then, as now, she kept her role in the tragedy a secret. She supposed they all thought she'd recovered over the years. She lived a normal life, held down a responsible job. But she'd never let another man get close to her.

She got up and went to the kitchen with Mason padding behind her. While she fixed a sandwich, she allowed herself the luxury of thinking about Joe Tarleton. He was the stable force in her life right now. She trusted him to help her prove that Rex Harwood had killed a woman before her eyes.

But what if Joe couldn't do that?

Would he still want to get to know her if he couldn't find the evidence she needed? Before she'd told him about Rex, Joe had definitely sent friendship signals, and she'd intercepted them happily, though she'd managed to keep her manner at its usual controlled level while butterflies held a sock hop in her stomach. Joe's response was unmistakable. He hadn't come to the gift shop's opening for the coffee.

She wondered what Joe believed. Why had he chosen to be a detective? What drove him to help people in trouble? What things would he die for? Did he believe God was real?

She stared at the sandwich. Her appetite had fled. It didn't matter what Joe believed about God or life or love. She needed to settle this herself. Lately her pricking conscience had told her she couldn't go on ignoring God. She wished she had someone to talk to about it. Bethany or Keilah would discuss it, she was sure. But they would be hurt to know she'd felt so cold and empty for so long. She didn't want pity, she wanted answers.

Slowly, she walked to her bedroom and to the bookcase. Her Bible was still there, in like-new condition. She hadn't touched it in twelve years except when she moved and when she dusted.

It slipped easily into her hands, and she stared down at it. Mason came to the doorway and yawned. She remembered the sandwich.

"Come on, fella." She returned to the kitchen and broke off a piece for him. "You can have half and I'll have half."

She sat down at the table and opened the Bible. The faint smell of leather tickled her nose. It had been so long, she had no idea where to turn, but she knew the answers she sought were in this book.

Turning the pages, she stopped at a place where her own handwriting was squeezed into the margin. Petra began to read.

An hour later, Mason came to her, his brown eyes large and trusting. Petra stretched.

"All right, boy. I hear you."

She went to the living room and pulled back the drapes. Smoke rose from behind the fence. She opened the sliding door just a crack and caught a whiff of grilling meat. If Rex was barbecuing, he wouldn't be roaming the neighborhood. She reached for the leash.

She walked swiftly at first, letting Mason pull her along. Somewhere in their first circuit of the park, she came to a decision. She would attend church on Sunday. It would be a start. Dealing with the past would be painful, she knew. Every time she remembered, it hurt. But she wanted more than anything to put things right with God. Maybe then she could address the other obstacles in her life—her job, her anxiety over Rex Harwood's crime, and her growing feelings for Joe. In all the years since the crisis that had driven her away from church and God, she'd proclaimed herself a crusader for truth. It was time to go to the source for truth. She headed Mason for home at a slower pace, tired but finally at ease.

Chapter seven

Joe got into the unmarked car Nick was using and buckled his seatbelt. Nick slid behind the wheel and started the engine.

"I'll take you back to your car, Joe. Sorry we didn't find anything that will help you much."

"Well, we've established that Mrs. Harwood is really Mrs. Harwood."

"Yes, I agree. Between my photo comparisons and what the neighbors who've known her longest say, I think we can rule out her being murdered two weeks ago." Nick looked over at him as he hit the turn signal. "But that won't help your client."

"True." Joe shook his head. "Don't get me wrong. I'm not sorry she's alive. I just wish you could have kept a lower profile making sure." He watched the residential section morph into a business district. Portland hadn't changed much since he'd lived and worked here. "I don't like to think anything is wasted. We learned a few things by asking if anyone noticed anything unusual."

"Oh, sure." Nick laughed. "We learned that a woman saw Mr. Kendall, across from Harwood, raking his lawn on what might have been the fateful day. That's supposed to be very unusual, since he's known as a lazy man."

"Yeah, but Kendall himself saw nothing odd. Of course, two people saw the squad car in Harwood's yard that night. That was unusual." Joe smiled and shrugged.

"Oh, don't forget the squirrel on the power line and the Nova Scotia car parked down the block. And one of Ms. Wilson's neighbors saw the Fed Ex truck come down Acton Street twice in one morning."

"Highly suspect," Joe agreed. "Of course, Mrs. Reynolds's statement that she heard Rex and his wife bickering once could be helpful."

"It's not much." Nick glanced at his watch. "Why don't you come have supper with us? I can call Robyn and let her know you're coming."

"Thanks, but I thought I'd stop off and see my client before I head home."

Nick sobered. "I've gotta admit, I'm leaning toward thinking the patrol officers were right. You can't make a body disappear into thin air. The guy is a professor, not a magician."

"Yeah, yeah." Joe stared out the window.

"I truly wish we'd found something, Joe. For your sake, for the client's sake, and so I could tell my sergeant he was smart to let me do this."

"I wish we had, too. But even more, I wish we could have gone to Harwood's and had a look at his family room."

"Don't start, Joe. You know it ain't gonna happen."

Petra slid the strap of her purse over her arm and walked past the nurses' station. Pulling out her key ring, she greeted the security guard near the emergency entrance.

"Heading home?" he asked.

"Yes."

"Want me to walk you to your car?"

"Thanks, Ed."

The sun still hovered above the horizon, and in the full daylight she wasn't frightened, but she wasn't taking any chances. Glancing ahead toward her car, she stopped short. Joe Tarleton was leaning on the hood of her red Avalon. A rush of pleasure sent blood surging to her cheeks.

"There's a friend waiting for me, Ed. Thanks a lot."

"Okay. Have a good evening."

She stepped forward eagerly. "Joe! What a nice surprise." A dark thought hit her. "That is, I suppose it's nice. Has anything happened?"

He smiled and took her hand for an instant. "I came down on business this afternoon, and I thought I'd hang around and update you instead of using the phone. More personal, you know?"

"Is this the kind of service you give all your clients?"

He grinned. "If I did, I wouldn't get much work done."

She grasped the implication—she was special. She liked that.

"So, what did you do in town?"

"I spent some time with my friend Nick."

She eyed him carefully. He gave her a half shrug, and she knew he wasn't going to tell her everything. "How is Nick?"

"He's good. Say, can we get something to eat? I'll bring you up to speed. I seem to remember a seafood place in the Old Port . . ."

"Sounds like fun. But I need to stop by my house and feed Mason and take him out for a few minutes."

"Fine. Can I follow you there?"

She couldn't keep her pulse even as she drove home. Every time she glanced in the rearview mirror she saw Joe's ten-year-old black Chevy and she knew that in minutes he'd walk into her kitchen. As she hit the button on her garage door opener, it struck her that she'd never brought a man home to this house. Deliverymen and cops didn't count. She'd lived here more than ten years, and in all that time she hadn't had a deep relationship with a man. Of course, this wasn't romantic. Joe was just going to wait while she walked the dog. He parked in the driveway, and she waited for him to enter the garage, then put the door down. Even for a few minutes, she wouldn't leave it open. As a single woman living alone in the city, she'd learned to take extra precautions she would have thought foolish twenty years ago, growing up in a small town.

She led him into the kitchen, and Mason danced joyfully around her, then stopped and leaned back on his paws, eyeing Joe with suspicion. He barked once, and Petra spoke.

"Take it easy. You've met Joe. He's a friend." She stroked the dog's head and motioned to Joe to step closer.

Joe crouched and held a hand out. Mason sniffed it and moved toward him, instant friendship gleaming in his liquid brown eyes.

"Hey, fella." Joe patted him firmly and scratched behind Mason's ears. "You're a good dog. Yeah!"

Petra smiled. "He's not much of a watchdog, but I love him. I'll just be a minute." She pointed to the counter. "Do you want coffee? It would only take a minute for me to start it."

"I can wait." Joe sauntered toward the living room doorway. "Can I take a peek at the backyard?"

"Sure." She hesitated but decided Joe would do best left on his own for a minute. "Make yourself at home. I'm going to change my shoes."

When she had left her nurses' shoes in the closet and donned sneakers, she put Mason on his leash. Joe walked to the corner with them and they circled the park together. Joe asked her where the Wilson family lived in the "old days," and they hashed over the changes Waterville had seen in the last twenty years.

"Why didn't we know you in high school?" she asked, brushing back her hair. The wind had picked up, and she wished she'd braided it.

"I went to Winslow High, across the bridge."

78

"Aha! There are some great old homes in Winslow."

"Yeah, there are, none of which the Tarleton family owned. We had an apartment over my father's furniture store." His smile was more of a wince.

"Are your folks still alive?" she asked.

"They split when I was a sophomore, and my father died a few years ago. My mother remarried and moved to New Jersey. Can you beat that?"

Petra chuckled. "Who would leave Maine for New Jersey?"

"Exactly."

"Well, our parents are both gone now," she said. "I guess that's why this invitation to move in with Bethany and Keilah has such a strong pull. I pretty much ignored my family for a while, and now I'm beginning to realize what I lost. I want to be part of it again. The camaraderie, and . . . maybe it sounds silly, but I want to belong."

"That's not silly." They walked in silence for a few minutes as they headed home. "So, you're thinking of moving up there with them permanently?"

"Yeah, I'm seriously considering it."

When they got back to her house, Joe offered to play catch with Mason in the backyard if Petra wanted to change out of her uniform.

After hurriedly changing into a dress, she glanced out the back window of her bedroom toward the fence. Joe was throwing a stick for Mason, and she saw no one in the Harwoods' yard. Still, the heavy feeling refused to leave.

After she fed Mason, they went outside and Joe opened the door to his surprisingly clean car for her. He drove to the restaurant without hesitation. It was one she'd taken Bethany and Keilah to when they visited her in Portland the previous fall. Joe didn't seem to mind the high prices, which she was certain were due in part to the restaurant's excellent view of the harbor. He turned out to be a charming conversationalist, and she put aside thoughts of their professional relationship and relaxed, enjoying sitting across from a handsome, articulate man. Why had she shut herself off all those years? She'd thought it was because she hadn't found a man who knew the meaning of honesty. Was it actually because she hadn't met Joe Tarleton?

Over the deep-sea scallops, he got down to business and told her how he and his friend Nick had spent the afternoon.

"We didn't learn anything that will support your claim. I'm sorry, Petra."

She frowned slightly. "I'm glad his wife is all right, but I can't help wishing you'd found something. I keep thinking about what he did." She shuddered. "Can't help it."

"And I keep thinking about *how* he did it," Joe said.

"What do you mean?"

"How he pulled it off. A woman's body is not an easy thing to hide. But he seems to have managed."

Petra stared down at her plate. "I've asked myself a thousand times where he put her, but nothing comes to mind. Did you get a good look at the back of his house?"

"Yeah. You've got a great view. What you saw must have been terrifying." Joe smiled and reached over to squeeze her hand. "Hey, let's let it go for now. It gave me an excuse to come down here to see you."

Her heart skipped. "You needed an excuse?"

He laughed. "Well, I really did want to talk to some people in the neighborhood and see what they'd tell Nick about the Harwoods. But I wasn't sure how you'd react if I just called you and told you the truth."

"Which is?"

He looked into her eyes with such intensity that she forgot where they were and why. His voice came out low and husky. "I've been wondering for the past few days if your eyes were really as green as I remembered. So when Nick called to tell me

80

he was going to follow up on the patrolmen's report on your case, it seemed like the perfect opportunity to come check."

Petra stared at him for a moment. She could feel a flush creeping up her neck. She wasn't ready to dive into a relationship, was she? Not until she knew him better. The memory of Danny's angry face flashed through her mind. Even so, her mouth refused to stay in a frown as she gazed at Joe. She struggled with it for a moment, but the smile won.

The deep gleam in Joe's eyes went from hopeful to ecstatic, and she felt her color deepen even more.

She took a sip of ice water and set the glass down. "Have you settled the question yet?"

"Oh, yeah. Greenest eyes I've ever seen."

His riveting gaze held her motionless for a good ten seconds. At last she forced herself to look away, a bit confused by her feelings. She studied her plate and began to eat her coleslaw, even though she considered it a miserable excuse for a vegetable.

When his last scallop and French fry had disappeared, Joe picked up his napkin and wiped his lips, leaving his dish of coleslaw untouched. "So." He leaned back and watched her chase her last scallop around her plate with her fork. "We should do something next weekend."

"Is that ethical?"

He blinked.

"To date a client, I mean." Suddenly she wondered if she'd mistaken his intent. Maybe he meant they should do something about Rex Harwood. If this went on, Joe would think she had a perpetually scarlet complexion.

His smiled widened. She half expected him to say something like, "Who's talking about dating?" Instead, he leaned toward her and dropped his voice. "I don't know of any rule against it, but if the thought makes you uneasy . . ."

"Maybe just a little."

"Nothing major, then. But we could get together when you're at your sisters' and talk some more. Maybe go out, if you're comfortable with that." He sat back looking a bit disappointed. His confidence seemed to have waned, and she hated that she'd done that to him. Just for a minute, she'd imagined what the future could be like with Joe. Why couldn't she have just said yes, and sorted it out later?

On the drive home, he renewed his pitch to have her get away from Portland, at least for a short while.

"I'd like to know you're safe until this thing is over. You don't need to stay here, so close to it. Nick Wyatt is on the detective squad with the Portland P.D., and if anything comes up, he'll tell me."

"Does he believe my story about . . . the murder?"

"I can't say for sure."

"You told me that you and Nick were both satisfied Mrs. Harwood is alive."

"Yes."

"So, if Rex did kill a woman, it wasn't his wife."

"Looks that way," Joe said.

"I wonder who she was."

Raindrops splatted on the windshield, and Joe turned the wipers on. Petra felt her stomach knot as she stared out the side window. Would Nick's interest do any good, or would it only infuriate Rex to learn the police weren't done with him yet? Surely one of the neighbors would tell him about the questions that were asked today. Imagining his anger brought painful images to mind. Rex killing again . . .only Petra was the victim.

She turned to see Joe's profile in the twilight. "Do you think I'm in danger?"

"I'm just saying, don't take any risks you don't have to. Until they get the evidence they need to put this guy away, keep your head down."

"But how can they get evidence? They tried and found nothing. Even your friend didn't make any headway. They're not going to keep the case open." Her helplessness to do anything about it frustrated her.

Joe shook his head. "They should have turned it over to the detective squad right away."

"Is that standard procedure?"

"Well, I'm guessing the patrol officers agreed there was absolutely nothing to your story. Otherwise, they would have."

"Don't they have to treat all complaints seriously?"

"Yeah. But, see, they felt they'd done that. So now what evidence may have been there is probably gone, or at least compromised."

He drove into her driveway and walked her inside the garage. She let her key ring hang from the lock on the kitchen door and turned to face him on the step. His dark eyes had taken on a mysterious glitter. Her heart surged in response, but she pushed down the reaction and worked hard for a pleasant tone that didn't give away her turmoil.

"Thanks, Joe. I enjoyed this evening."

"Me, too. You be careful, okay?"

"I will be."

He bit his lower lip and nodded. "All right. You're a big girl. Just remember, you can call me anytime."

He reached up and touched her cheek for an instant, and she drew in a shaky breath. His fingertips were warm, inviting. Would he kiss her if she gave him a little encouragement? She wasn't ready for that. Still, the idea warmed her. She couldn't meet his eyes. If she did, she might send him a signal it was way too soon for.

The moment was over. He stepped back a little and smiled.

"I'll see you next weekend," she said.

"Yeah." He walked outside. When his car began to roll, she hit the button to lower the overhead door, then turned the knob on the kitchen door. For once, Mason hadn't barked, but she thought she heard him whining.

"I'm coming, boy," she called as the door swung open. She flipped the light switch.

Mason lay on the floor whimpering. His pleading brown eyes fixed on her as he writhed on the linoleum.

Chapter eight

"Mason, baby, what's wrong?" Petra knelt beside the dog and petted him. He lay on his side, staring mournfully up at her, and let out a moan.

"Are you hurt?" She stroked his belly gently and he whimpered.

She looked around quickly. Nothing out of place in the kitchen. Could he have gotten into something harmful? She rose and hurried through the house, checking each room. Nothing stood out as a possible cause of Mason's distress. His supper bowl was empty, and the water dish still held a half inch of clear liquid.

She yanked open the drawer where she kept her phone book and looked up the veterinarian service's emergency number. Her vet's office was closed, but the woman who answered told her to take Mason to a veterinary hospital a couple of miles away, and the on-call doctor would meet her there. She wished Joe were with her, but there wasn't time to call him now, while every second mattered.

When she urged Mason to get up, he started to roll over as if to get his feet under him, then lay back, whining. It was all she could do to heft his heavy, squirmy body and lug him out to her car. She managed to brace him against the back fender while she opened the door, and after much pushing and prodding she had him settled on the blanket she kept in the back for him. She decided not to try to buckle his canine seatbelt harness, as its pressure might cause him more agony.

She drove carefully, so as not to disturb Mason and not to attract attention. The last thing she wanted now was to be stopped by a traffic patrolman.

A man and a woman came out of the veterinary hospital pushing a small stretcher.

"I'm Dr. Vincennes," the man said. Petra opened the back door of her car, and he stooped to give Mason a quick initial exam, then lifted the dog onto the stretcher.

Inside the lobby, the woman told her, "You can sit down out here while the doctor tends your dog. I'll bring you some papers to fill out."

Twenty minutes later, Petra paced the waiting room from the chairs to the curtained window and back. If only she'd opened the kitchen door before Joe had left, he'd be with her now. Again she thought of calling him, but she didn't feel she could ask him to come back because her dog was sick. He'd be late getting home as it was.

She could hear the murmur of low voices. If someone didn't come and tell her something soon, Petra felt she would explode. She eyed the closed door warily. She could barge in there. What was the worst they could do to her?

She turned back to the window and peeked out at her car in the parking lot. What was that verse she'd read last night? It seemed ages ago, but barely twenty-four hours had passed since she'd read chapter after chapter of scripture and poured out her heart before God.

"And the peace of God, which transcends all understanding, will guard your hearts and your minds in Christ Jesus," she whispered. She had recognized the verse when she read it as one she'd memorized years ago in Sunday school. Who'd have thought she could pull it out after so long? Peace was something she'd lost long ago, but she hadn't realized she missed it. The past few weeks were nothing but turmoil. Working way too much. Seeing her sisters again, hearing their pleas to move in with them, followed by the horror of witnessing a murder, then the whole unsavory business with Rex Harwood. Even meeting Joe had added tension to her life. And now Mason was ill. She wasn't sure she could hold up much longer if Mason died.

"Dear God, please don't let me lose my dog." Tears sprang into her eyes. Was a sick pet worthy of God's attention?

The door behind her opened, and she turned. The woman came out, her face grave.

"Dr. Vincennes says you can come in now."

Petra followed her into the exam room. The doctor was washing his hands, and Mason lay quietly on the stretcher. She walked around it, afraid of what she would find, but her heart leaped when she saw the dog's tail twitch.

His large, brown eyes gazed at her, and he whined. Petra petted his sleek head.

"Hey, fella. Are you okay?"

The doctor turned toward her as he dried his hands. "I think he'll make it, Miss Wilson, but I'd like you to leave him here overnight for observation, if you don't mind."

"Sure. What . . ." She cleared her throat. "What's wrong with him?"

The doctor stepped up to the opposite side of the stretcher and laid a hand on Mason's flank.

"It's a good thing you got him here when you did. I'm sorry to say it, but there's no question. He was poisoned."

Joe braked as a truck merged into his lane. As much as he'd enjoyed seeing Petra again, he'd be glad to get home after this long day. Another hour behind the wheel. That would make it after eleven when he got to Waterville. He yawned and signaled to change lanes. He was about to pull over and pass the truck when his cell phone rang. He groped the passenger seat, where he seemed to recall tossing the phone when he left Petra's house.

"Yeah?"

"Joe? Mason's been poisoned!"

"What? Petra? You talking about the dog? No!" Outrage rushed through him like a freight train, setting every nerve on edge.

"Yes! When I went in the house, he was rolling on the floor, obviously in pain, and I took him to the vet. They pumped his stomach. He's really sick, Joe."

"Call the police."

"I . . . I can't. When I told the vet Mason stayed inside alone while I was out, he implied that I must have left something toxic where he could get into it. The police won't come here again. And if they do, they'll say I was careless, or maybe they'll accuse me of deliberately poisoning him myself. Joe, I . . . I can't call them again. Not for this."

He glanced at the clock on the dashboard, but it hadn't gotten any earlier. He sighed. "Hang on. I'll be there in forty-five minutes."

"I can't ask you to do that."

"You didn't ask. I'm doing it."

"But you must be nearly home."

"No, I'm not." He signaled for the Topsham exit. "Are you at home?"

She hesitated, and her voice seemed to have shrunk when she said, "I'm sitting in my car outside the veterinary hospital. They're keeping Mason overnight, but I'm afraid to go home. Joe, I've never been scared like this before."

"Well, there's no way I could sleep if I went home knowing you were alone when something like this has happened. Isn't there a fast-food place a couple of blocks from your house?"

"Y-yes."

88

"Just drive down there and go in and get some coffee. I'm on my way."

By the time he passed the Yarmouth exit twenty minutes later, he'd calmed down somewhat, but then the fatigue hit him. He punched the cruise control up another notch. Of course, he didn't want to get a ticket, either.

Petra's words went round and round in his tired brain. Was there any possibility she was making it up? He'd seen her with her dog. She loved him. Joe couldn't swallow the theory that she'd poisoned the perky dog's supper. He'd stood right there and watched her scoop the food out of the bag and into Mason's dish. Still, his training as a police officer cautioned him to keep an open mind. Never rule out anything. Follow the evidence.

He sighed, recognizing the need for expert advice.

Okay, Lord. I maybe haven't come to You as often as I should lately. What I need right now is wisdom. That and some energy. Let me get there in one piece, and help me to see the truth.

Ahead he saw a cruiser on the shoulder, lights flashing. A pickup was stopped in front of it. As soon as he was safely past it, Joe increased his speed again. That trooper, at least, had his hands full.

He reached the McDonald's at last and hurried from the car to the door. At least they were open late in the big city. The burger joints in Waterville would be closed now.

Petra stood as soon as he entered, her lovely face creased with worry lines. He wondered if she'd been holding back tears for an hour.

When he reached her, he folded her in his arms, no questions asked. He felt her body rack with a sob, and he held her, ignoring the stares of the two young men in the corner booth. He rubbed her back gently, inhaling her faintly floral scent and feeling the green dress's smooth fabric.

She held on to him for a good thirty seconds, then pulled in a huge breath and stepped back.

"Thank you. You really didn't have to come back."

"Sure I did. You can't go into the house alone, and you can't bring yourself to call the police."

She swallowed hard. "I'm sorry. I should have done that, I guess."

Joe shrugged. "I'm not sure I blame you. Come on, let's get you home."

She turned and picked up a covered cup. "I ordered this for you ten minutes ago. I hope it's not cold."

He punched open the lid and took a sip. "Perfect."

She smiled then, a wobbly, watery smile, her green eyes swimming.

"Thanks." It came out gruffly. He wrapped one arm around her and hustled her out the door. "You go ahead. I'll be right behind you. When you get to the house, if everything looks normal, go ahead and open the garage door."

She nodded.

He chucked her under the chin gently, like he would a child. "It's going to be okay. You got it?"

"I got it."

She slid into her car. It only took a couple of minutes for them to drive to her house, during which Joe downed half the coffee. The street was quiet, and all the houses were dark. The residents in this upper-middle class neighborhood had real jobs to go to in the morning, and on weeknights they turned in early.

Petra drove into the garage, and Joe parked outside and walked in to open her car door for her.

"Is the house door locked?"

"Yes."

"Give me your keys. You can stay out here if you want until I check the house."

"No, I'd like to come with you."

90

"Okay." He unlocked the kitchen door and pulled his pistol from his shoulder holster. Petra's eyes flared, but she said nothing. He entered cautiously, feeling her close behind him. After checking the kitchen, coat closet, utility room and living room, he told her to remain by the dining table while he swept the rest of the small house. Guest room, closet, hall bath. Petra's room, another bath, closets. Bedroom-turned-study, where she kept her computer and hundreds of books. Another closet.

He went back to the kitchen. "Any basement?"

"No, just a crawl space."

"Inside entry?"

"No."

He nodded and holstered his pistol. "I'd say you're clear. I didn't see any trace of a forced entry, but I'm not equipped to do a thorough investigation in the middle of the night."

She exhaled heavily and put a hand to her forehead. "Thank you, Joe. I feel so . . ."

"Hey, none of that. You're exhausted. You need some sleep."

"Isn't there anything we can do?"

"You told me you didn't find anything that could have poisoned Mason."

"That's right. The doctor will send a sample to the lab and they'll try to find out what did it."

Joe rubbed his scratchy chin and stifled a yawn. "Tell you what. I'll come back here in the morning and see if I find anything."

"You can't go all the way home tonight and then drive back here."

"Maybe I'll call Nick and see if I can crash on his couch for a few hours. But there's one other thing we can do now."

"What's that?"

"We can pray."

Petra lay awake long after Joe left. How could this have happened? No way had she left out something that would harm Mason if he ingested it. The alternatives made her shiver. Had someone slipped him something deliberately? But when? And how? She found herself straining to hear any strange sounds above the pattering rain.

She prayed again, silently, repeating the words Joe had offered, but in choppy, disconnected thoughts. *Lord, protect me. Take away my fear. Keep Mason alive. Help us to learn the truth.*

Her digital clock glowed with large, red numbers. She rolled over, away from its light. Rain spattered louder against the window, and she puzzled over the enigma of Joe Tarleton. Until tonight, she had no idea he believed in God, yet he prayed like a seasoned believer. Somehow, it fit with everything else she knew about him. A surprise that seemed obvious once you knew it.

She lay inert, between sleep and consciousness. She hadn't relied on God in more than twelve years. She'd moved away from her family and the embarrassment of facing them daily, but not away from her pain. She'd avoided church and spiritual introspection. Was the perpetual heartache she'd endured the result of her aloofness from God?

Joe hadn't hesitated to suggest they pray together. Had she mentioned to him that she and her sisters went to church last weekend? Bethany and Keilah very likely mentioned God and church to him, and he must assume she was a believer, too.

Memories assailed her with more wakening power than strong coffee. She saw Joe, steady and dependable, responding immediately to her need. She shouldn't have hesitated to call him. And he would be back in the morning. That was a comfort. She had only to make it through a few more hours of darkness.

In contrast was the specter of Danny, who had failed her and then left her feeling guilty ever since. Or was that guilt self-imposed? Danny probably hadn't intended to crash into the Belgrade information booth with his truck and end his life that night, and if he had, he surely didn't do it just to dump guilt on her. The timing did that. After she confronted him about the drugs, if he'd waited a week to get himself killed, she wouldn't have hung on to the self-condemnation all these years.

The verse from Philippians nudged her again, like skywriting in her brain. *And the peace of God, which transcends all understanding . . .*

Might that peace still be possible for her? Maybe the guilt she carried wasn't necessary, though she'd made it an appendage that went with her everywhere.

Lord, if I can have that peace, show me. I'm tired of blaming myself. And I'm tired of being alone.

The rain beat on the window, and sleep claimed her at last.

Joe jerked awake and opened one eye. Two a.m. He stifled a groan and shifted in his seat. Rain thumped on the roof of his car. Terrific. The passenger-side window was no doubt leaking again, and the floor mat on that side would be drenched by morning.

He sat up and arched his spine. Maybe he should just crawl into the back seat. But sleeping deeply would defeat his purpose. He squinted into the gloom and took a hard look at Petra's house. He itched to creep around to the back, but two things kept him in the car. First of all, he didn't want to get soaked and shiver all night. More importantly, she might be awake, too, and if she heard him sneaking around, as edgy as she was right now, things could go south in a hurry.

The clues, few as they were, cycled through his mind for the thousandth time. One eyewitness, whom the patrolmen had found less than credible. One upstanding citizen who argued occasionally with his wife. If Harwood just kept quiet, he could get away with murder. The problem was, Petra wouldn't keep quiet, and that's what would bring him down. Even if no one believed her, Harwood couldn't take the chance. Someone might decide her story had merit and reopen the case.

The neighbors. Joe had told Nick how important it was to keep a low profile, but Nick had wanted to talk to all the residents who lived near Harwood. Somebody on the street must have told Rex or his wife about the two men who came around today asking questions. Plainclothes cops. That would set a guilty man off. Harwood had bluffed his way out of the initial investigation. So far, so good. But Petra hadn't given up, and now some detectives were on it.

Joe thought about what he'd do if he were guilty. He'd try to send the witness a message that wouldn't incriminate him. Shake her up a little. And if that failed, he'd have to shut her up. The mugger in the parking lot. That had flopped, if it was indeed Rex Harwood. All right, so he went for the dog. Hurting Mason would not only drive it home to Petra that she'd better keep quiet, but also it would remove her best warning system. If her dog died, there would be no barking to alert her if he sneaked over the fence to silence her.

Joe pulled in a deep, slow breath. He hated that scenario. Was it his own fault Mason had been poisoned? He'd begged Nick to take the case seriously, and this was the payback.

One other possibility wouldn't quit nagging at him. He didn't want to examine it closely, but he had to.

Petra could have imagined the parking lot scare. Her nerves were frayed, and she saw a man out there and felt frightened. What if he didn't really chase her? What if he had no weapon, but was holding the keys to his own car? Or what if he simply didn't exist? And what if Petra imagined—or made up—the night noises and the non-messages on her phone? In that case, how was Mason poisoned? Joe decided he would call the vet himself in the morning, just to be sure. The idea that

Petra might have told him a wild story sickened him. She wouldn't. She couldn't. And if the dog wasn't at the vet's, where had she stashed him? In a kennel? Or worse? No, he wouldn't believe that for a second.

But he would make the call. Just so he could tell Nick he'd covered every possibility.

The street stayed quiet. One car had rolled by since he took up his vigil. He leaned his seat back a notch and yawned.

Chapter nine

The doorbell's chime woke Petra and she sat up, her heart racing. Who would call this early? And why wasn't Mason barking his head off the way he always did when the front doorbell rang?

The past night's events came back to her in a rush. Mason. The vet. Joe.

Joe!

She sprang out of bed, grabbed her robe, and tore into the kitchen. Standing on tiptoe, she peered out the window over the sink, through the filmy curtain. Joe's black car was in her driveway. The bell chimed again, and she went to the door and opened it a crack.

"Hi."

"Hi." His smile was a bit apologetic. "Sorry. I thought maybe I could take a look around before you go to work, and I didn't want to frighten you if you heard me poking about."

"That's fine. I'll get dressed and make some coffee. Did you have breakfast at Nick's?"

"Uh, no."

"Eggs and toast okay?"

"Fantastic."

She nodded and smiled. "I can open the garage if you want."

"Yes, please."

She shut the door and locked it, went through the kitchen to the connecting door, and opened it. She pushed the button to raise the overhead garage door, then ducked back inside. As fast as she could, she slapped a coffee filter and two scoops of Green Mountain into the basket of the coffeemaker. Everything else could wait until she was dressed.

Fifteen minutes later she took possession of the kitchen once more, feeling presentable in her uniform and more coherent. She saw no sign of Joe, but his car was still out front. Once she had the frying pan out and the table set for two, she detoured into the living room and pulled the drapes.

Joe knelt just outside the patio door, using a magnifying glass to study the deck where it abutted the house. He looked up at her and grinned. Petra unlocked the door, removed the broomstick she kept in the track for double insurance, and slid the door open.

"Good morning. Coffee's ready."

He stood up and brushed off the knees of his khakis, but slightly muddy wet spots marred the fabric.

"Smells wonderful. Should I come in this way? The grass is still wet, and I don't want to mess up your rug."

"It's all right." She hesitated. "Or do you think . . ." She looked down at the carpet. "Did you find anything? I mean, if someone came in this way . . ." Her pulse accelerated. She'd known the possibility existed last night, as soon as the vet said the word *poison*. But the actuality of a person—a particular person—entering her home and hurting Mason terrified her. How could he have gotten in here without leaving evidence behind?

"Not this way," Joe said.

She stood back and tried to stay calm. "Come on in, then."

He stepped inside. "I think your little track jammer made things more difficult for your visitor." He nodded toward the broom handle she'd laid aside. "Too many people don't take that precaution."

"So, no one came in here?"

"I didn't say that."

He followed her to the kitchen. Petra poured him a mug of coffee, and he leaned against the counter watching as she melted a dollop of butter in the frying pan and cracked three eggs into it.

"Runny or hard?" she asked.

He chuckled, and the lines at the corners of his eyes crinkled. "You've never been a waitress, have you?"

"Nope. What should I have said? Sunnyside up?"

"I'll take mine over easy, thank you."

"Not me. I like mine well done." She poked the yolk of the egg she'd mentally designated as her own and let it run and congeal. "Joe, do you think this is related to the murder I saw?"

"It's a strong possibility."

"Then you think Rex came over here and poisoned my dog?"

"I haven't ruled it out."

Her hands trembled as she opened the bread bag and put two slices in the toaster. "What do I do? Can we convince the police he was here?"

He sipped his coffee then said, "We may never be able to prove Rex Harwood murdered anyone, but I suspect we'll be able to prove someone broke into your house last night and harmed your dog."

"Really?"

"The rain was pretty heavy in the night, but there were some indentations in the ground under a window on the west end of the house. Maybe footprints, maybe not. I think it's the room where you have your computer. It's a window that's not completely hidden from the street, but in the dark it would take a sharp-eyed passerby to notice anything. I'd like to take another look inside that room this morning."

"Sure. Anything." The fear that had dogged her since last night made her chest hurt when she inhaled.

"I'll check more closely in the laundry room, where you keep Mason's food, too. If I find evidence of breaking and entering, we should be able to make a good case to the police that someone was here last night while we were at dinner."

"You don't think it could have happened earlier, when I was at work?"

Joe shook his head. "Mason was fine before we went out to eat. Bright eyes, lots of energy. I suspect whatever laid him low was a fast-acting poison, but I'd like to talk to the veterinarian about it."

"They may not have the lab report back for a few days."

"Okay. But you're going to call this morning anyway, to check on Mason, right?"

"Yeah." Petra glanced at the clock. "I'm not sure when they'll be open. It's not seven yet."

Joe was eyeing her with a thoughtful, brooding expression.

"I guess I could call the emergency number again if they don't answer the regular phone."

"What's the name of the pet hospital? Maybe I could swing by there after you leave for work."

She gave it to him, and his brow cleared at once.

"So you don't mind me talking over Mason's case with the vet?"

"Of course not."

His dimple came out when he smiled. Petra's stomach did the little flip. She turned back to stove to hide the confusion he'd caused. The eggs were starting to stick to the pan.

"Oops, looks like they're over but not easy. Sorry."

"That's okay. I'll get the toast before it burns, though."

"What, you like that rare, too?"

They sat down together smiling. Petra caught her breath. "Would . . . you like to ask the blessing, Joe?"

"Sure."

His simple prayer of thanks resonated in her heart. She knew she'd found at least part of what she had lost. She was

100

thankful for so many things—Joe's presence, a new day, and Mason's life. For the first time in a long time, she wanted to give thanks.

When they had finished eating, Joe went out to his car and came in with a briefcase, which he carried into her study. Petra cleaned up the kitchen. It was nearly time for her to leave for the hospital.

Joe came into the room as she hung up her dish towel, and she turned to him eagerly. "Did you find anything?"

"Not much. A small clump of soil on the rug in there, but it's so small I can't say it proves anything."

"He would have come in before the rain started," she mused.

"Probably. Was that window locked?"

She started to answer, but then she caught her breath. "I think so, but it's possible that it wasn't. It was warm last week. I was in there one evening, using the computer, and I opened the window to get a breeze through. I try to keep all the windows locked, but . . . I guess I could have forgotten."

"Well, it was locked when I checked it last night. If he came in that way, he most likely locked it behind him and went out the front door. Let's take another look at Mason's food."

They went into the utility room, and he examined the bag of dog food and Mason's dishes.

"Do you keep chemicals in here?"

"Just laundry detergent and bleach. Well, stain remover, furniture polish, stuff like that."

"Show me where."

She opened the cabinets beside the dryer.

"And nothing was open when you came in and found him ill?"

"No, everything was the way I always leave it."

He nodded, looking from the cabinet to the mat where the dog dishes rested. "Nothing could have spilled in his food accidentally. I'd like to try for fingerprints on that windowsill in the other room and the doorknobs and Mason's food dish, if you don't mind."

"You can do that?"

"Sure."

"Okay. Then what do we do?"

"Not a whole lot if I don't get anything solid. We don't want to upset Mr. Harwood again. If I were still a cop . . ."

"You were a cop?" She stared at him, and Joe's eyes flickered. She should have guessed. He had his own fingerprint kit, and his best buddies were police detectives.

"Well, yeah." He set his briefcase on the washing machine and opened it. "I'll need your prints, too, for comparison."

Petra watched him with a growing certainty that he didn't want to discuss his past as a police officer.

"So, what would you do if you were a cop now?"

"Well . . ." He took a plastic case from the briefcase. "I'd beg my boss to get me a warrant so I could go over Harwood's family room properly."

"Thank you, Joe. You know you're the only one who believes me."

"Well, you haven't told many people. I'm sure if you told your sisters and your friends, they would take your word for it."

"I don't know."

He eyed her keenly. "You know what you saw, right?"

She thought back to that night. The grisly image was still terrible, but not as vivid as it had been.

"Of course I do. And I keep reminding myself that if there was an innocent explanation—like two people practicing for a play or something like that—he would have told the police immediately. But he didn't. The best he could do was suggest I'd seen a movie playing on his big screen TV, as if I'd fall for that."

Joe nodded. "It's because of your memory and the specific details you gave me that I believe you."

Tears filled her eyes. "I wish I hadn't seen it."

"I know. I wish you hadn't, either." He stepped toward her, and she found herself once more in his warm embrace. The strength of his arms around her brought more comfort than she could have imagined. For a moment she wished she could stay there and not face the day before her, but she knew that wasn't possible.

She straightened and cleared her throat. "Do you want to take my prints now? I need to get to work."

"Sure."

He took out an ink pad and a card and reached for her hand. Her pulse pounded, but she wasn't sure if it was because of Joe's touch or the thought of Rex Harwood coming in here and trying to kill her dog. She winced, and Joe looked up at her.

"You okay?"

Petra nodded. "Yeah. Just thinking. Can you lock up when you're done?"

"No problem." He pressed her fingertips to the card and rolled them, one by one, then released her hands. "All set."

She went into the kitchen and washed her hands.

"Petra?"

"Hm?"

Joe stood in the utility room doorway. "Okay if I take a little of Mason's food to the veterinarian?"

"If you want."

He shrugged. "I just thought it might help them if they saw what was supposed to be in his stomach. There have been cases where whole lots of dog food were poisoned in the manufacturing process."

"Yes, I've heard of that happening. Do whatever you think is best, Joe."

"Man, that's a lot of bad luck for one person," Nick Wyatt said.

Joe paid for coffee for both of them, and they carried it to a booth. "I know. Thanks for meeting me. I wanted to bring you up to speed."

"You should have called me last night. You could have stayed at my house."

Joe stirred a packet of sugar into his coffee. "I'd have worried about her."

"So, the dog was actually poisoned."

"No question. I spoke to the vet myself. He even let me see the pooch. He looks okay now—a little droopy, is all. Petra can pick him up tonight. But the doc said if she hadn't brought him in pronto, he'd probably be dead."

"That's tough," Nick said. "But you didn't find any evidence of a break-in at her house."

"Nothing definite. And no prints except Petra's."

Nick studied his face. "Is this getting personal?"

Joe put off answering for a few seconds by taking a sip from his cup. But Nick wouldn't let him off the hook. They knew each other too well. "Maybe."

"Watch yourself, Joe."

"Right."

"No, I'm serious. This could haunt you if she's stringing you along."

"She's not."

"You don't know that yet."

Joe sighed and stirred the coffee again. "Look, I can't prove she saw a murder, but I believe her. She's telling the truth."

"Could be. And could also be she thinks it's the truth but it's not."

"You think she's nuts? You've never even met her."

"Sorry. I'm just saying. You know?"

"I know." Joe scowled. His coffee still tasted bitter. He reached for another packet of sugar.

That night Petra brought Mason home. He entered the kitchen warily and sniffed all around before padding into the utility room, turning around three times, and flopping on his cushion.

Petra squatted beside him and patted his smooth head.

"Poor puppy. Glad to be home and in your own bed?"

She checked on him frequently throughout the evening. Mason seemed too tired to play. Now and then he gave a loud sigh. The vet had told her not to feed him until morning, but she made sure he had cool, fresh water available.

The whole house felt subdued. She found herself stiffening and listening for any strange sound. Finally she turned on the television, something she rarely did anymore. Twenty minutes into the program, she realized she had stopped paying attention and lost the thread of the story. All she'd been thinking about was Rex Harwood and how much she hated living close to him. Time to change that. She shut off the TV and went for her phone.

Bethany didn't answer her cell phone. Surprised, Petra tried the number for the gift shop. Keilah's weary voice answered on the third ring.

"Tarleton Detective Agency."

"Keilah? It's me."

"Petra? Oh, sorry. I thought it was another call for Joe."

"What are you doing at the store so late?"

"We're restocking and cleaning." Keilah yawned audibly. "Sorry again. We're almost done."

Petra went to the patio door and looked out. Observing the Harwoods' house was becoming a habit. Lights shone over there tonight, but she didn't see any movement.

"You two are overdoing it. Are you there at eight o'clock every night?"

"No, but some new merchandise came in, and Bethany interviewed clerking applicants all day. We've been busy, which is good, but it means we have to catch up on mundane stuff in the evenings. We sold every one of those painted slates, can you believe it? The artist is bringing us a dozen more tomorrow."

"Well, do you two still think you need another roommate?"

"You mean you'll come?" Keilah's voice rose at least an octave.

"I'm starting to think I'd like to change to a new job and get out of the city. It would take me some time to sell my place here, though."

"Well, sure, but you could give it over to an agent. Oh, Petra, that's fantastic. Do you want to help us in the shop?"

"I think you'd better hire someone, and fast, before you're both completely worn out."

"A lot of summer people are coming in."

"That's good," Petra said. "Maybe I can check with the Waterville hospitals to see if they have any job openings posted."

"Sure. How soon do you think you can move permanently?"

Petra sat down in a chair, relieved now that the decision was made. "I'll talk to my boss Monday. I'll have to give two weeks' notice. It'll probably take longer than that to tie up loose ends, though." All sorts of flotsam sailed through her mind. *How will I move all my stuff? Will Mason make the adjustment all right? I'll need to find a good vet right away.*

Keilah's voice bubbled at her again. "Oh, I can't wait to tell Bethany. She's out back."

Petra caught a little of Keilah's excitement herself. Moving in with her sisters would be good for all of them. She wished she could tell them everything, but that thought was still too unsettling. Too much had happened. Bethany would be terribly upset. "So, Joe's getting a lot of calls on the line in your shop?"

"More than I expected," Keilah said. "I've got a half dozen messages for him right now."

"I'm sorry. Maybe you should tell him it's too much."

"No, we're glad we can help, and he seems to be getting more work now. He's promised to hire a new secretary. Say, you wouldn't want to—"

"Absolutely not. I've seen Joe's office, and I'm pretty sure he can't afford me. I'll settle for an ER, thank you. But hey, I'll tell you something. Joe and I went out last night."

"Really?" Keilah's response was almost a squeal, and Petra smiled.

"Yeah. He was down here on business yesterday. I'll tell you about it when I see you."

"You'd better. So you're coming tomorrow?"

"Well, I'm supposed to go to a seminar in the morning."

"For your job? But if you're going to quit . . ."

"I'll think about it," Petra promised.

She went to the utility room and knelt by Mason's bed. He licked her hand.

"Hey, fella. Want to sleep in my room tonight?" He wagged his tail and hauled himself to his feet. She dragged his bed down the hall to her room and arranged it on floor by the far side of the bed. Mason immediately lay down, sprawling on his side and staring up at her.

"Just stay there and be comfy," she told him. "It's okay."

Looking around, she tried to estimate how many boxes she would need for books and clothing. Dishes, too. The idea of uprooting herself and starting over daunted her, but she felt free. She could leave behind the fear.

Or could she?

She took out her pajamas and walked to the window. She couldn't help looking over the backyard again. A single light shone upstairs in the Harwoods' house.

I'm not running away. I want to do this.

Once she'd made up her mind, Petra couldn't wait to pack. After a lot of thought, she had called the evening head nurse at the ER and asked her to leave a message telling her supervisor she would not attend the seminar the next morning. A flurry of packing followed, and she anticipated driving to Waterville early Saturday with a load of her belongings.

Suddenly, she stopped and eyed the top of her dresser. In spite of the jumble of small items she had created there, she had the distinct feeling that something wasn't right. She stood motionless, going over the collection of cosmetics and toiletries.

"Mason, what's missing?"

The dog yipped.

She smiled at him. "Feeling better, aren't you? Good boy!" She stooped to stroke his head.

It came to her. She straightened slowly, staring at the dresser.

"My extra key ring." Her mouth went dry and a pang of fear jabbed her.

She sorted through all the junk on the dresser top, then opened each drawer and checked to be sure the keys hadn't dropped into one during her packing frenzy. *Jewelry box!* Maybe she'd tucked it in there to get it out of sight. But only her costume jewelry and the box that held the ill-fated engagement ring lay inside. She lay down on the rug and peered under the dresser. At last she stood and pulled it away from the wall, checking carefully behind and beneath it.

She pushed aside a pile of clothes and sat down on the edge of the bed. After a moment of thought, she went to her study and checked her desk drawers. Next she got her purse from the kitchen counter and upended it on the table. The key ring she normally used was there, with a fat bunch of keys, including several she couldn't remember the locks for. Her stomach did a rapid descent as she surveyed the collection she'd carried around with her.

Mason came and stood at her knee, watching her with his head to one side.

"You think I'm crazy, don't you?" Petra asked, feeling inside the slender inner pockets of the leather purse.

Nothing. She cradled her head in her hands.

Think! When did you last see it?

That was the trouble. She couldn't recall seeing it. For months it had lain on her dresser untouched. The longer she thought, the more certain she was that it had been there last week when she went to Waterville for the gift shop's opening. And when she returned? She wasn't positive. The possibilities frightened her.

She frowned at Mason, who had lain down at her feet and was licking his front paw.

"It will turn up," she said without believing it.

He looked up at her and whined.

Chapter ten

After stopping at her sisters' gift shop the next morning to pick up a key to their house, Petra drove the two miles to her soon-to-be new home and unloaded her boxes and luggage. Mason romped about the big lawn, and she took a few extra minutes to play with him. It felt good to be out in the sunshine without wondering if a killer watched her.

She and Mason rode back to the shop, where she plunged into the activity. The store was full of patrons, and Bethany stayed glued to the cash register while Keilah scurried about to help customers. Petra settled Mason in the back room with a rawhide chew and approached Keilah.

"What can I do?"

"Answer the phones. Joe ran an ad in the paper for the secretary job."

She fielded calls, careful to keep Joe's messages clear and accurate. Between them she ran to the back room at Bethany's request to find a new roll of cash register tape and start a pot of coffee.

Joe wandered in about three in the afternoon. Petra spotted him as soon as he walked through the door carrying a covered plastic platter. Her heart soared. He grinned and disappeared into the back room. When she joined him a few minutes later, he was pouring a mug of coffee. On the card table sat a tray of fresh fruit and cheese.

"Your sisters told me to quit bringing them pastries." He put the mug in her hands and reached for another.

"This looks great." She helped herself to a slice of honeydew.

"I'm glad you called me last night. Did your keys turn up?" he asked.

"No."

"Did you sleep all right?"

"Not too badly. I was glad Mason was with me."

"What was on the key ring?" Little ridges creased his forehead, and the dimple was hiding.

She shrugged. "Car and house keys. But I might have moved them and forgotten." She watched his face, hoping for reassurance.

"Do you think that's what happened?"

"No."

"I don't like it."

"Me, either." She squeezed her lips together to keep from saying, *He was in my house. He stole my keys.*

Joe set down his mug. "You need to change the locks."

"I . . ." She looked away, feeling stupid. Rex Harwood could be ransacking her home this minute. "You're right. I'll call a locksmith from work on Monday and set it up. Maybe he can come that night, when the real estate agent is going to look at the house."

"You're selling, then?"

She nodded. "Not just because of this. I want to."

"I know." He finally smiled, a gentle, wistful upturn of his lips. "I'm glad."

She wondered if his opinion was formed objectively or on a more personal level.

Keilah dashed in. "Hey, is the coffee ready? There are only two customers out there and Bethany ordered me to take a break. Oh!" She screeched to a halt and scrutinized the fruit platter with a look of adoration on her face. "Joe, something tells me you got a fat paycheck. Your snacks are improving."

Joe laughed. "Stuff yourself." He looked quickly at Petra. "Not you. I'm hoping you'll join me for dinner later, and I want you to have at least a semblance of an appetite."

"Just one more." Petra took a toothpick and speared a chunk of fresh pineapple. She closed her eyes and smiled as she chewed the tart, juicy fruit. She should probably decline dinner and insist they talk business in his office or the living room at the house. Keep it professional for now. But she didn't want to.

"Well," Joe said. "Next time I want to impress a woman, I'll send her fruit." He winked at her and filched a piece of melon. "Oh, by the way, I've hired a secretary. She can't start 'til a week from Monday. Can you stand it another week, Keilah?"

Keilah looked up at him with a strawberry in her hand. "Barely."

Joe laughed and drained his coffee cup. "You've been a big help. I'll see you later, ladies. Pick you up at six?" he asked Petra.

"Sure."

The next two hours flew by. Just as Bethany locked the door and turned the Open sign to Closed, the phone rang. Petra dived for it and put the receiver to her ear.

"You Shouldn't Have."

Only silence greeted her. After a moment, a click was followed by dial tone.

She dropped her jaw and stared at the receiver. Keilah burst out laughing.

"What?" Petra asked in a sharper tone than she intended. Had Rex Harwood learned of her connection to the new gift shop?

"I'll bet that call came on Joe's phone." Keilah nearly doubled over as she chortled. "Imagine calling a detective and hearing, 'You shouldn't have.' I'll bet you scared them to death."

Petra looked down at the phone and let her shoulders sag. She replaced the receiver carefully and managed to chuckle.

Dinner with Joe on his home turf was even better than dinner with Joe in Portland. The restaurant wasn't as upscale as the one in the Old Port, but it won her over with candlelight, soft music, and perfect steak. Their conversation faltered now and then, and Joe looked at her in what she felt was appraisal.

"I guess this is kind of strange for both of us," she said. "At least, it is for me. It's been so long since I got close to anybody."

"Yeah, me too."

"Do you think this was a bad idea?" She watched him closely, almost afraid of his answer.

Joe shrugged. "It would be nice if the case could be put to rest. Maybe then we could think about other things. What we want our relationship to be when it's over."

"Yeah." She knew there was more behind it than the professional-client thing. Maybe it was her own hesitance, or maybe it was something more on Joe's part.

After dinner he drove down Main Street and curved around onto Front Street, the one-way that paralleled Main but went the other direction.

"Why are we going this way?" Petra asked softly. "I know you know where the house is. You picked me up there."

"It's a beautiful night." He smiled at her as they passed the newspaper office. "Thought we might take a little stroll." He turned into a parking lot on the riverbank. "I used to walk across here when my mother needed something from the store." He parked the car close to the end of the Two-Cent Bridge.

"I haven't been here for . . . I won't say how long." Petra laughed. "I used to love to walk over this bridge. Bethany was

114

terrified of it, though. We went out in the middle once, and she froze up and wouldn't let go of the railing. I thought I'd have to carry her home. I finally told her I was going to run over to the police station and ask an officer to come get her, and that did it. She was more afraid of being alone on the bridge than of walking over it."

"I wonder if she's still afraid of it."

"I don't know. She's changed a lot since she married Mike and lost him. She's stronger in a lot of ways. I'll bet she'd walk right over it without flinching now. If the water wasn't too high."

Joe smiled broader and opened his car door. Petra reached for her door handle, but waited. She shut her eyes for an instant, knowing he was walking around behind the car to her side.

Thank you, Lord. Thank you for this moment.

He opened the door and she got out. When he took her hand, it seemed right. Maybe this was the time for her to get past her reservations and open her heart again.

The rushing of the river was the only sound as they walked out onto the footbridge. Joe led her to the center of the span and leaned with his forearms on the railing, facing downstream toward the railroad and automotive bridges over the Kennebec.

"I used to love to watch trains go over the bridge from here," he said.

Petra inhaled deeply. The moonlight turned his dark hair to silver and reduced the distant streetlights and vehicle taillights to fireflies. A cool breeze lifted her hair. Joe straightened and slipped his arm around her. She wasn't cold, but he was so deliciously warm that she nestled in against him and rested her head on his shoulder.

"Thanks for bringing me here," she said.

"I don't like your leaving Mason here with your sisters when you go back."

She turned her head upward and looked at his face. "I won't have to worry about him while I'm wrapping things up at work and packing and showing the house."

"And you won't have him at night when you're alone."

She looked out over the river. "That's true. It's a tradeoff. But if anything else happened to him . . ." She pulled away from him and turned to meet his gaze head-on. "Joe, what else can I do? I'm afraid if I have any more contact with Harwood, this thing will escalate. I just want to move out as quickly as possible."

Joe took a long, slow breath and looked up at the sky. "I'd like to go down there again and hang around campus, maybe find some of his students. I thought about it before and got sidetracked."

"What's the point?"

"A man who kills in a rage like that must have a short temper. There must be people who've seen him lose it before. Maybe in the classroom."

She considered that for a moment. "School is out for the summer."

"Mmm. There are probably summer sessions. But you're right, it's bad timing. I could look into his wife's background."

"She wasn't even there when he did it."

Joe was silent. She wondered if he heard her over the sound of the swirling water.

After a long moment his gaze met hers. His dark eyes gleamed with intensity. "Something in me won't let this go. It's in my blood, or my training, or my nature, I don't know."

She laid her hand on his sleeve. "I want justice, too. But I don't want Mason, or you or me, to be hurt."

"Come on."

He turned back toward the parking lot, and they walked slowly across the bridge holding hands. Petra paused at the end and looked back along the narrow decking, then up at the moon. Joe waited in silence until she moved again. When they reached his car, he opened the door for her, then went around and got in.

"Tell me about your training," she said softly as he held up his keys in the dim light.

He stuck one into the ignition but didn't turn it. "What do you want to know?"

"Everything."

He sat still, staring toward the river, and she almost regretted asking, but she needed to know more about him, needed to know she could trust him completely. This was the standard she had set for the man she could love—total honesty.

"I was with the Portland P.D. for three years."

Portland. Of course. He was at ease in the city because he'd patrolled those very streets.

"Nick Wyatt was my partner. Best friend. We did everything together. Went through the Academy together. I was his best man."

"You quit the force, and he stayed with it."

Joe nodded, not looking at her. He sighed and leaned back against the seat. Petra waited. Was she asking too much of him?

"We had an incident. I decided to . . ."

They sat in silence again, and Petra didn't want to push him any further. The possibilities intrigued her, but she knew she didn't want to push at this stage of their budding relationship.

"Joe." She touched his hand. "I'm sorry. Forget I asked."

"No, it's . . . If you want to know, then you should know."

"I don't have to. Everyone has painful things in their past."

"Do you?"

Touché. She inhaled and let the breath out carefully. "Yeah."

"Do you feel like talking about it?" he asked.

"No."

He nodded. "Okay." He turned the key in the ignition, and the engine sprang to life.

"Wait."

He looked at her, his eyebrows arched.

"Joe, what does it mean if we can't talk about our past? Does it mean we don't know each other well enough yet, or . . . does it mean we've built walls we never intend to break down?"

After a second's pause, he flexed his shoulders. "You got me."

She reached over and turned the engine off.

"Twelve years ago, when I was twenty-three, I found out my fiancé was dealing drugs. I turned him in to the police. He..." She coughed, but the lump in her throat stayed put. "I told him I'd made the call. Stupid of me. We had a huge fight. He hit me and stormed off just before the police arrived. I found out later they chased him, and he crashed his pickup into the information booth in Belgrade. DOA. At least no one else was hurt." She stared across the river at the old Scott Paper mill, stark and imposing in the moonlight.

Joe stirred. "I remember that. I was at the Academy."

Her eyes filled with burning tears, and she put her hand to her forehead. "Just don't tell me you went to the scene. That would be too freaky."

"No. The instructor told us about it in class. How not to conduct a high-speed chase."

"Danny went out with a big bang. I never told my family about my part in it." She realized she clutched the arm rest with a death grip. "But I've always felt guilty that by calling the police I played a part in Danny's death."

"Hey, it wasn't your fault," Joe said. When she didn't respond, he added, "They've got a new information center in Belgrade now," Joe said. "It's better than the old one."

An involuntary chuckle shook her. "I don't think I want to visit it, thank you."

"Sorry."

They sat in silence for a long time. Petra let the tears flow down her cheeks.

Joe's warm fingers touched her hand and wrapped around it.

"I hate that you went through that." His low voice cracked, and she flexed her fingers to squeeze his hand gently.

She wiped her cheek with the back of her free hand. "I was a big fool. There were warning signs all over the place, but I ignored them. I loved him. I trusted him. And I refused to believe anything bad about him until the proof stared me in the face. Ever since then . . ." She shook her head and sniffed.

Joe leaned forward. "There might be some Burger King napkins in the glove box."

She tried to hold back a giggle. It came out a muffled burble. "Thank you. I'm all set." She reached for her purse and dug out a packet of tissues.

Joe sat back while she tried to repair the damage to her face and blessed the darkness that would hide the worst of it.

"Does your fiancé's family still live in the area?" he asked.

"Yes. Keilah told me his sister came into the gift shop yesterday. That's something I've got to be ready for. If I take a job at one of the hospitals here, the day may come when I walk into a patient's room and have to look his mother in the eye. She probably still blames me."

"Why should she?"

"I've blamed myself for twelve years. Why shouldn't she?"

"Oh, please. It's your fault he got into crime and decided to lead a bunch of cops on a chase? It's your fault he lost control at ninety miles an hour and wrecked? You're just lucky you weren't in that truck."

His sharp tone startled Petra, and she couldn't frame a suitable reply. Her chest throbbed as she tried to breathe evenly without sobbing. A puff of air escaped in a spasm, and she turned her face to the window.

After a long moment, Joe sighed. "I can see why you didn't want to talk about this."

"You're the one who didn't want to talk," she reminded him.

"Yeah, well, you know what bothers me the most?"

"No."

He reached over and touched her chin, turning her face gently until she looked him in the eye. "We're so much alike. We both have things that keep us from going forward, even when we want to."

She sat still for a second, then put her hand up to cover his. "I thought maybe it was my situation that bothered you."

Joe smiled faintly. "I wish this murder was solved. I wish a lot of things. But it's not just that. Nick would say I have cold feet. I've never quite been able to form a permanent relationship with a woman." He sat back. "I saw a lot of pain in the past, and it's hard for me to risk going through something like that."

"Things you saw at work?" she asked.

"Oh, yeah, that, and at home." He looked out toward the river for a moment. "My folks had a messy breakup. The stuff they put each other through . . . I promised myself a long time ago that I would never do that to a woman."

"That must have been hard for you as a child," Petra said.

"Hard? It was impossible. When my father finally left, it was a relief. I hate to say that, but it's true."

Her heart filled with grief for him. "Joe, I don't want to sound trite, but you're not him. And you don't have to be like him."

"Yeah." He inhaled deeply. "You asked me about my time with the P.D."

"You don't have to talk about it."

"No, maybe it's better if I do. Nick and I were called for backup one night for a couple of officers who had responded to a robbery in progress. Nicky was driving, and we got there a minute too late. Both officers were killed."

He sat in brooding silence. Petra felt the regret and shame pour off him.

He looked up. "I couldn't stop going over it in my mind. If I'd been driving . . . If we'd taken a different street . . . If we'd taken our supper break at point A instead of point B . . ."

"You couldn't have gotten there faster than you did."

"Yes, we could have. If I were convinced otherwise, I think I could have handled it. We had counseling. I decided I didn't want to be responsible in a case like that ever again. So I turned in my badge." He rubbed both sides of his face. "I should take you home. This conversation isn't helping either of us."

"Wait. I disagree."

He cocked his head toward his shoulder and eyed her cautiously. "You do?"

"Yes. Why was Nick able to stay with the job and you weren't? It was what you'd always wanted to do, wasn't it?"

"Well, yeah. But Nick . . . he's got a different temperament from me. He's a good cop. A very good cop. And he can live with that."

"With being a very good cop?"

"Yeah."

"But you couldn't."

He didn't answer, and Petra raised her chin.

"I see. You have to be the perfect cop. Nobody dies on your shift."

"Something like that."

"Did you get all A's in school?"

"No."

"Then what makes you think you have to be perfect at being a cop?"

121

"We're talking lives here."

She studied his face. "So you went off on your own to work by yourself. No one telling you you're not good enough or fast enough or smart enough. No more life-and-death crises. A guy like you can help people without feeling guilty. But, Joe, a very good cop, even though he's not perfect, can do so much good."

"I didn't claim it was logical." He started the car.

During the ten-minute ride to the house, Petra almost spoke several times. Was he feeling that he couldn't be a perfect husband or father either, and so he had avoided marriage all these years? She kept her silence. Anything she could say, she knew Joe had probably told himself thousands of times already.

Lights shone from the living room, kitchen, and one upstairs bedroom of the big house. When Joe opened her door, Petra got out.

"It's a great house," he said.

She nodded. "They gave me the tower room."

"They must want you bad to bribe you like that."

She smiled. "It's good to be with them. I missed . . . love."

He walked her to the porch. "Petra, you shouldn't hang around with guys like me."

"Why not?"

"I'll feed your melancholia. We should be asking ourselves how God fits into all this and what He would want us to do."

A lock of his hair had fallen down across his forehead, and she smoothed it back. "You're right. I've sort of started over with God recently, and I'm sure He doesn't want me worrying over this. He promises peace."

Joe nodded. "I've prayed about my situation a lot over the years, but I keep fretting over it. I need to let it go."

"And go back to being a cop?"

"No. My agency is finally taking off, and I like it."

"Then you should keep doing it." She hesitated. "Maybe we could help each other. I'll pray for you, and you pray for me."

"Yeah. Go to church with me tomorrow?"

"I'd love to."

"Good. Your sisters can tag along if they want."

He stooped toward her, and Petra caught her breath. His lips met hers and she stood still, except for her pounding heart. He slowly enfolded her in his arms, and she slipped into a dreamy haze of content.

Suddenly Mason barked inside the house and light flooded the porch.

Joe pulled back and eyed the closed door. "Next thing we know, your father will yank that door open and say, 'What are your intentions, young man?'"

She laughed. "If we'd met in high school . . ."

"Yeah, well, we've met now."

He stepped back, and Petra reached for the doorknob.

"Thank you, Joe. I'll see you in the morning."

She went inside thinking not about the bleak past, but about the future's possibilities.

Chapter eleven

Nick's call late Monday afternoon caught Joe by surprise. He had been on the go since early morning and had the satisfaction of wrapping up a missing persons case. Returning to the office after three o'clock, he garnered messages from Keilah and set up appointments with several potential clients. Word was getting around the upper-crust of Waterville. If you had a sticky problem that needed discretion, call Tarleton Detective Agency.

"Joe, I just wanted to check with you on Petra Wilson's case. Anything new?" Nick asked.

"Nothing except that her extra key ring is missing. I'm afraid the person who poisoned her dog took it. I told her to change the locks pronto. The dog has recovered, though."

Nick sighed. "Okay. I'm sorry you couldn't find anything that would get us a warrant when you went over her house. Well, I've got to run over to the airport and check out an abandoned car."

"Since when is the hotshot detective squad investigating dumped cars?"

"The airport manager's antsy. They had a bomb scare last month, remember? Now they've had a car left in the short-term parking for two weeks. The officers on duty at the airport are trying to trace the owner, but it's a Canadian license plate, and it may take a while to make contact."

"That's a job for airport security and the patrolman they have out there."

"What can I tell you? The airport manager called the chief, and the chief is sending me. They want it taken care of today, and no publicity if it's a non-story. The public has a long memory for things like 911."

"How long did you say it's been sitting there?" Joe asked.

"Couple of weeks. Look, I gotta get moving. But it sounds to me like it's time for you to deep-six that bogus murder case."

Joe's mind reached back for an elusive piece of information, but he was distracted by Nick's last remark. "Hey! There is nothing bogus about Petra's case."

"Okay, okay. I've got to go, although it's probably a case of someone parking in short-term when they should have left it in long-term. Still, you get a car with Nova Scotia plates, and—"

"Hold on!"

"What? I really need to hustle."

"What day was the car left at the airport?"

"Does it matter?" Nick asked.

"It might."

"Uh . . . the eighteenth."

"That's it!" Joe leaped up from his chair and flipped back the pages of his notebook.

"What's what?"

"Nicky, Nicky. Remember our little stroll through Rex Harwood's neighborhood last week?"

"Yeah."

"The Nova Scotia car, remember?"

After a pause, Nick's voice came, muffled. "Hold on. I'm looking for my last notebook. One of the neighbors mentioned a car, but it wasn't near Harwood's house."

"No, it wasn't. It was parked a block down the street, so we discounted it."

"I dunno, Joe. People go back and forth from Portland to Nova Scotia all the time on the ferry. That's what we have The Cat for. Folks ride over to Yarmouth on the catamaran, spend the day sightseeing, and come back."

"Nick, think! The vanishing body. The patrolmen checked Harwood's car, but they didn't check every car parked on the street."

"You're stretching it, Joe."

"Prove it."

"What was the name of the woman who mentioned that?"

"Eileen McAdams," Joe roared, staring at the name in his own notes. "Did they pop the trunk yet?"

"No, they're waiting for me to get there."

"Small blessings. Get over to the airport and call me from there!"

Joe rolled out of bed at five the next morning and got an early start. He parked in front of the Portland police station just as Nick arrived for duty.

"You going over to interview Harwood's neighbors again?" Joe asked him without the usual civilities.

"Yeah. By the time we finished at the terminal last night, it was too late."

"Can you give me a ride-along?"

Nick frowned. "Yeah, I guess. Wait out here."

Joe leaned against his car and watched the uniformed officers going into the building. He thought about Petra and the weekend they'd spent together—idyllic if one overlooked the ragged discussion of their pasts and fast-forwarded to their sweet goodnights. Sunday was an all-around good day, the best he'd had in years. Church with Petra and her sisters, followed by a home-cooked dinner and a lazy afternoon sitting on their front porch and playing catch with Mason.

A passing police officer recognized him and stopped to chat for a minute. At last Nick returned, and they headed for Harwood's street in an unmarked police car.

"The clump of hair I found in the trunk of the car last night is definitely human," Nick said as he drove.

"I knew it," Joe said. "I'm telling you, this is how he got rid of the body. He carried it out to her car and drove down the street a little ways."

"And none of the neighbors noticed?"

"Apparently not. Did you tell your sergeant about the possible connection to the murder Petra witnessed?"

"I told him. He's not buying the theory yet, but he agreed I should check it out."

At the McAdamses' house, Nick rang the bell, and again Joe let him be the spokesman.

"Yes, I remember the car," Eileen McAdams told them, "but it's been a while. Let's see, it was down there when we came home from the movies that night." She pointed to a shady spot by the curb between her house and the next one on the block. "I figured the Dales had company."

"We checked with them, and they didn't," Nick said. "Can you describe the car for me again, ma'am?"

She grimaced and stared off down the quiet street. "I didn't think it was important. Let's see, it was light-colored. Maybe tan or . . . or silver."

Joe said nothing, but he recalled his notes from the previous week. She'd said then the car was white. But after all, it was after dark when she saw it.

A young man approached the doorway from behind her.

"'Scuse me, Mom. Gotta get going."

"Okay. Have you got your phone with you?" Mrs. McAdams stepped aside, and her tall, blond son eased past her. Nick and Joe retreated down the steps.

"Yup. Catch you later." He nodded in the general direction of the two officers.

"Hey, Will, wait a sec," his mother called, and the young man stopped on the walkway and turned around, his eyebrows raised.

"These gentlemen are detectives. Remember, I told you they were asking questions a few days ago?"

"Oh, sure." He took an uncertain step back toward them.

"You saw that car that was parked over by the tree a couple of weeks ago, didn't you?" she asked.

His face clouded. "What car? Mom, you've got to be more specific."

Nick told him, "This was the evening of May seventeenth. Your mother told me the family went to a movie together to celebrate your sister's birthday."

He nodded, still frowning.

"Do you remember a strange car parked down there when you came back from the theater?" Nick asked.

"The one from New Brunswick," Mrs. McAdams said.

Joe almost spoke but caught himself.

"Oh, that one." Will McAdams threw his mother an indulgent smile and said to Nick, "It was Nova Scotia."

"Are you sure?" his mother asked.

"Yes, Mom. 830 JHP."

Joe barely succeeded in keeping his jaw from dropping. He spoke for the first time. "Tell me that's the plate number."

"Yeah. 830 JHP."

"He has a good memory," his mother said.

Nick flashed a look at Joe.

"It was my girlfriend's birthday," Will said.

Nick's brow wrinkled. "I thought it was your sister's birthday."

"Not the day. The license plate. My girlfriend's birthday is August thirtieth, and that was the plate number. And J for Jessica—her name."

Joe smiled. "What's the HP for?"

Will grinned back at him, clearly pleased. "My new Hewlett-Packard printer."

His mother came down the steps. "Things like that are a game to him. I told him he should be an accountant, but he's majoring in phys. ed. Can you believe that?"

Five minutes later, Nick had extracted all the pertinent data he could get from the young man, and Will went on his way to his summer job.

"It's the car that was left at the airport, all right," Nick confirmed as he pulled out of the McAdamses' driveway. "I'll get back to the police station and get on the computer. We're still trying to contact the owner in Nova Scotia."

"Or the next of kin?" Joe asked grimly.

Nick gritted his teeth. "Yeah."

"I think you'll find the owner didn't get on a plane that day."

"If there was a body, he got rid of it before he took the car to the airport." Nick shook his head. "Could be anywhere."

"Oh, so you believe me now. The woman Petra saw strangled was in the trunk of that car."

"I'm not married to the idea, but it's worth a second date. Look, we still don't have enough for a warrant on Harwood. We have nothing to connect him to the car. No prints on the steering wheel, for instance. If the car's owner is missing, we'll have to see if we can get some DNA from the family. Working back and forth over the border, that could take some time. But if we can match the hair from the trunk to the car's owner . . ."

"Go for it," Joe said.

"What are you going to do?" Nick asked.

"I'm doing some work on another case today. I've got a meeting in an hour. Then I'll try to do some more background on Harwood. I did quite a bit of research on his family last week, but this Nova Scotia connection puts a new twist on things. I'll go over to the library and use one of their computers. We need to know what his link is to Nova Scotia."

Several hours later, Joe left the library with the papers he had printed tucked neatly in his briefcase. His meeting had run longer than he'd anticipated, and he'd had to cut the library time short. He'd previously pinpointed the location of the Harwood family home, where Rex grew up, in Sidney, between Waterville and Augusta. Apparently the father moved away after Rex's mother died, and Joe's attempts to trace him had so far been a dead end. He remarried, Joe was certain. Rex was only eight when his mother died. The father must have remarried and relocated, but so far Joe hadn't turned up the details.

He glanced at his watch and realized Petra would be off work in an hour. He wanted to see her again. They both knew they still had issues to overcome, but spending time with her couldn't hurt, could it?

His stomach rumbled. He'd worked through the normal lunch hour before he thought of food and then grabbed a hot dog and coffee, but it was barely a memory. He decided to eat a candy bar now, make a few calls on his other cases, and stick around long enough to see Petra. He wished he could whisk her away from Portland until this was over, but she was determined to work out her last two weeks at the hospital. Somehow he'd have to make sure she survived it.

Petra's phone rang as she turned in to the residential neighborhood. She flipped it open and put it to her ear.

"Hello?"

"Hey, want to get something to eat with me? Nothing fancy tonight."

She laughed. "Joe! You're really coming all the way down here again so soon?"

"Oh, yeah. I'll meet you at your house."

"Okay, what time?" She signaled and turned onto Acton Street.

"Oh . . . about 5:18?"

She glanced at the dashboard clock, which read 5:17, then peered down the street. A black car was sitting in her driveway. Her spirits soared.

"Great! Just give me time to change and get rid of the detective in my yard."

She exited her car a minute later smiling.

"How you doing?" Joe asked.

"Good. Even better now."

"Can you stand a cheeseburger tonight?"

"If you want to save money, I can feed you here. Salad and a ham sandwich?"

"Deal."

He followed her inside, and Joe said at once, "How's Mason doing?"

Petra smiled. "I miss him. Bethany says he's making himself at home up there. I'd like to think he misses me a little."

She put Joe to work making coffee while she changed from her uniform into jeans. When she walked into the kitchen, she found him peering into the refrigerator.

"More leaves than the arboretum in there," he muttered.

"I eat a lot of salad."

He nodded skeptically, and she laughed.

Petra began to make the sandwiches, and Joe leaned against the counter.

"They found a car abandoned at the airport."

She froze and looked at him. "And?" She knew he wouldn't be here telling her this unless he had a good reason.

"And the same car was parked a block from Rex Harwood's house the night you saw the murder."

She stared at him. "Okay. What does this mean?"

"It means the police are looking into it. Could be related to the murder."

"But . . . they found a car today? I don't get it. How did they connect it to the crime?"

"The police were notified yesterday by the airport parking lot manager. Nick was assigned to check it out. He and I made the connection from our interviews in the neighborhood last week. Someone had seen a car that matched this one's description."

"Where has the car been for the last two or three weeks?"

"Sitting in the short-term parking lot at the airport, I guess. The ticket from the lot was on the visor over the driver's seat. It was parked there the eighteenth."

They sat down, and Joe asked the blessing. Petra thought about the new evidence as she took a bite of her sandwich.

"Did they find any fingerprints on the car or the ticket?"

"All I've heard so far is, none on the steering wheel. The airport manager thinks it's strange it was left there, but not critical, now that the cops have checked to make sure there was no bomb in the trunk. Just a nuisance for him. But if it's broadcast on the six o'clock news tonight, Harwood should find it very interesting."

"Why would they broadcast something like that?" Petra asked. "It's hardly newsworthy."

"I know, but a reporter showed up while Nick and a couple other officers were going over the car. The airport had a bomb scare not long ago."

Petra nodded. "I remember. You sound sure that Rex has something to do with this car."

"I think it's a good possibility," Joe said.

"You mean . . . the body. Wait a minute, there wasn't a body in the car, was there?"

"My first thought, too, but no."

"Then what?" Petra asked. "He used this car to get rid of it?"

"It makes sense. He made sure the body was out of the house and not near enough for the police to notice the car that

133

night. Her car might have been in his driveway when he killed her, but he moved it before the police arrived." Joe picked up half his sandwich. "Right now, authorities in Nova Scotia are trying to locate the owner. Nick called me an hour ago and said that so far they haven't been able to do that, but they're still trying."

"The owner of the car lives in Nova Scotia?"

"Yeah."

Petra shook the bottle of salad dressing. "Strange."

"Petra, I'm sorry to worry you with this, but I thought you should know. I've been trying to find something connecting Rex to Nova Scotia."

She nodded. "Could be a colleague in the academic world."

"Maybe." Joe put a small pile of vegetables on his plate and scowled at the bottle of low-calorie French dressing.

"I may have a bottle of ranch in the back of the fridge." Petra stood and opened the refrigerator.

"Rex has been waiting for this news to come out for weeks," Joe said. "Something to do with the body or the car. I mean, if he left the car there, he's been waiting for someone to try to locate the owner. He's probably been biting his nails to the quick wondering what's taking so long."

"Why would he want the police to find it?"

"To put an end to the waiting. If the case is treated as a standard missing persons case, he'll breathe easy."

"Why?"

"The car is too new to be abandoned intentionally unless it's connected to a crime or an accident. Right now the assumption is that the driver should have parked in the long-term lot but wasn't thinking and left it in short-term by mistake. Or possibly the driver took a flight out of Portland, got delayed somewhere and couldn't come back for the car as planned. But if it gets out that detectives found human hair in the trunk of the car . . ."

She slammed the refrigerator door and faced him with the bottle in her hand. "Did they?"

He flinched. "I'm sorry. Should have broken that a little more gently, I guess. But, yes, Nick Wyatt found several human hairs on the carpet in the trunk—more than you would normally expect to find there. Follicles intact, and the lab thinks they can use the DNA."

"Yeah, that would worry Rex, all right."

Joe nodded. "Nick is in charge of the case now. If this goes where I think it's going, you'll be his star witness when Harwood goes to trial. And Harwood will realize that. So you need to be extremely careful until this investigation is over."

She shivered. "But . . . are they going to arrest him?"

"Not yet. They don't have enough evidence to even say for sure there was a murder. Nick's trying to keep it quiet until they do. Nobody on Harwood's street seems to have seen the car at his house, but it was noticed later in the evening, down the block. If Harwood gets an inkling of what the police suspect, he'll get nervous. Petra, you've got to take some precautions."

Her knees wobbled, and she sat down hard. "I can't believe they finally found some evidence."

"Possible evidence. Could be nothing."

Her appetite had fled, but Joe continued to eat his sandwich. When he finished, he eyed his portion of salad for a moment, then reached for the ranch dressing with a resigned sigh.

"You don't have to eat that."

"I want to. Really."

She smiled, but sobered as her thoughts returned to the murder and the abandoned car. "Makes me feel a little jumpy."

"I debated on whether to tell you or not, and I decided you need to know. Petra, I'd feel a lot better if you moved to Waterville now. Tonight."

"I can't."

"What's stopping you?"

"You know I have to work."

"Call in sick."

She winced and looked down. "I can't do that. I mean, they're so shorthanded as it is, and now I'm quitting. I feel a strong obligation to finish out my notice."

"Okay." He stabbed a forkful of greens, looked at it for a second, and shoved it into his mouth. Petra almost laughed.

He coaxed her into finishing her meal, and when she put their few dishes into the dishwasher, he came to stand close to her.

"I'll ask you one more time. Please come to Waterville tonight."

"No."

He nodded. "That's what I expected you to say. All right, I'm going to make you a hotel reservation."

"Joe, that's not necessary."

"You got the locks changed, right?"

"Yes."

"I still think you should go to Waterville. Pack a bag, and I'll take you to your sisters'."

"Oh, stop it! I have to be at the hospital at seven tomorrow morning. You said Rex will lie low and wait to see how the police react when they find the car, and how the media presents it."

"Fine. You want to watch the news? It's almost time. Let's turn it on."

His dark eyes held a challenge. She inhaled deeply and led the way to the living room. They sat down together on the couch, and she turned on the TV. When the local anchor came on the screen, she turned up the volume. They listened carefully through the major headlines and local events. The weatherman gave his report, and the sportscaster began his. Near the end of the broadcast, the anchor gave the merest mention of a mysterious found car at the airport. "The car was searched, and

136

nothing dangerous was uncovered. The police have impounded the car and are still trying to locate the owner in Canada."

Petra hit the off button and turned to Joe, her eyebrows raised.

His square jaw seemed to protrude more than usual. "Okay, so they treated it like it was nothing. I still don't like you staying here. You don't even have Mason."

"But Rex will think he's safe now. If that was the way he got rid of the body, he's sitting over there thinking, *Yes! I did it!*"

"Doubt it. He's still trying to second-guess the police and you." Joe got up and walked to the patio door. He stood with his hands in his pockets, looking across toward the back of the big brick house.

Petra went to stand beside him. "What are you thinking?"

"I need to see inside that room."

"It's not going to happen."

"Why not?"

She seized his wrist, suddenly afraid. "Joe, you can't go sneaking around over there. That would really upset him. It could even get you in trouble."

"The drapes are open." Joe stooped and pulled the broomstick out of the track on her door frame. "Let's go out on the deck."

"What if they see us staring?"

"I haven't seen any movement in there. They're probably not home."

Petra's nerves flared as he unlocked the door and stepped outside.

Joe leaned on the railing, peering intently at the other house. Petra looked around, but saw no one else in the neighborhood who might be able to see them. Still, her pulse raced.

"You said the woman was holding something, and after he choked her, he picked it up."

"That's right," Petra said. "He put it up on a shelf."

"Can you see it now?"

"I . . ." She squinted toward Harwood's glass door. "I'm not sure. It was on the left, up high. Do you see something like a vase?"

"I've got binoculars in my car." Joe straightened.

"No! All we need is for them to see us spying on them with binoculars. Rex would have *me* arrested."

Joe frowned. "I'm going over there."

Petra felt as though her heart took a momentary leave of absence. "You are not!"

"They don't know me from Adam."

"What if Mrs. Harwood saw you talking to the neighbors last week?"

"I didn't go with Nick when he checked her out, and I was careful when we went around the neighborhood."

She swallowed hard. "What will you do?"

"Ring the bell. Tell them I've read all the professor's articles, which I have, and would love to talk to him about his method of dating porcelain artifacts."

She eyed him for a long moment. "You think you could pull it off, don't you?"

"I know I could."

"You'd pass yourself off as a scientist?"

Joe shook his head and guided her back into the living room. "I'm not going to lie to him. I'll represent myself truthfully, as an interested amateur. Academics love to talk about their pet subjects. I'm his biggest fan, and I've been wanting to meet him. He'll practically give me his lecture course for free."

She took a careful breath. Her chest hurt. "It's too dangerous."

"No. Either he'll let me in and we'll be best buddies in ten minutes, or he'll slam the door in my face. Assuming he's home. If he's not . . ."

138

"If he's not, you come right back here. Immediately."

Joe pursed his lips and shrugged. "There's one thing I want you to do."

"I'm not going over there."

"No, I wouldn't ask you to. But I'm going to get my binocs. You can stand here behind your curtains with them and watch. If you see me in there, you pay attention. I'll try to get him to show me the things on the shelves. You watch, so you can tell me which one the woman was holding when he killed her."

"You . . ." She bit her lip.

"It'll be fine. I promise."

"You'll mess up any fingerprints on it."

"True. But I have a feeling he wiped it off that night, anyway. And if you see the one she was holding, call me on my cell phone. I'll use it as an excuse to leave."

She felt a sudden desperation that frightened her. *If anything happens to Joe. . .*

"I can't stop you, can I?"

He bent close and whispered in her ear, "Nope, but you can pray for me." He kissed her on the cheek and headed for the door.

Chapter twelve

Joe parked at the curb in front of Harwood's house and got out of his car. He had considered walking over from Petra's house, but if the professor saw him arrive on foot and wondered where his car was . . . Nope. Better to let his vehicle be seen than to risk being linked to Petra.

He eyed the brick house as he ambled up the walk. It could use a little maintenance; the shutters needed repainting and one drainpipe had disconnected from the gutter. But it was a nice house, probably at least fifty years old, and the front lawn and perennial beds looked cared for. He pushed the doorbell and looked around.

The door opened, and Joe turned with a smile in place. A woman of about fifty faced him, her gray hair escaping from beneath a limp bandana. She wore a calico apron over slacks and a knit top.

"Mrs. Harwood?"

"Yes." She looked down her nose at Joe, and he smiled bigger.

"Would the professor be home this evening?"

She looked him up and down. Joe was glad he'd worn a suit.

"And what is your business with him, may I ask?"

"My name is Joe Tarleton. I live up in Waterville, and I was down here on business today. I've been wanting to meet

Professor Harwood. I'm a great admirer of his work, and I took a chance of coming by and possibly finding him home. I hope I'm not intruding."

"Actually, he is at a faculty meeting tonight. They're starting summer classes Monday."

"Ah." Joe grimaced. "That's too bad. I've read all Professor Harwood's articles, and I was so hoping I'd have a chance to talk to him about the expedition he's making this summer."

"Are you an archaeologist?"

"No, but I've been interested in it since I was a kid. I've been reading up on the ruins in Morocco. That is going to be a fascinating trip."

"I'm sure he'll be sorry he missed you," she said.

Joe turned on the high voltage smile. "I don't suppose he'll be speaking in the Waterville area soon? I would just love to catch one of his talks. In fact, I'd drive down here to hear him."

"Well, he often speaks in the Portland area, and I believe he's going to Camden next week." She stepped aside. "Why don't you step in? I'll get you a copy of his schedule. If you can attend one of his lectures, I'm sure you'll have the opportunity to meet him afterward. Most of the societies he speaks to hold a reception after."

"Oh, that would be terrific." Joe grinned and stepped into the entry. "I appreciate your doing that for me. It would—Oh!" He looked around the foyer and focused on a pottery mask displayed on the wall. "Is that one of the professor's artifacts?"

"It's a copy of a find his crew made in Mali. One of his favorite pieces. They sell copies in the gift shops at the Portland Museum of Art and the Maine State Museum."

"Indeed? That is just gorgeous." He glanced about, orienting himself. "This is a lovely home, Mrs. Harwood."

"Oh, thank you. I'll just get that schedule, if you'll excuse me. I believe he has copies in his study."

She left him, and Joe tiptoed a few steps toward what he calculated was the door to the family room on the back of the house. Sure enough, there were the glass doors and the big-screen TV.

"Here you go, Mr. Tarleton."

Joe whirled. She'd moved faster than he'd anticipated, even though she'd taken a second to remove the apron.

"Excuse me. I couldn't resist taking a peek at your charming living room."

"Oh, we have a formal living room. This is what folks call a family room. We relax in here."

"I can see why. It's beautiful, but cozy. And the pictures! Are those your children?" He gestured toward several framed photographs hung above a spinet piano.

"Yes, those are our three. And of course, we have grandchildren."

"Grandchildren?" He smiled and shook his head. "I bet they're wonderful."

"Oh, yes. We don't get to see them nearly often enough." She stepped down into the room, and Joe followed. "This is Caleb." She took a small pewter-framed picture from a shelf. "He's nine, and he plays soccer."

"Handsome boy," Joe said.

"And this is his sister, Madison. She's seven, and just the brightest little thing you ever saw."

"Oh, she's adorable."

Mrs. Harwood smiled and replaced the frame on the shelf. Joe pointed to a vase. "Now, that looks similar to some pieces that were recovered on the Crete expedition."

"Right you are." She smiled at him. "You weren't kidding me when you said you've followed Rex's career."

Joe shrugged. "I've always admired people who do the kind of work your husband does. Do you ever go with him on his trips?"

"Why, yes, I usually go out for at least a few weeks." She was beaming now, and Joe kept the eye contact and smile wattage going. "I get right down in the dirt with the students and sift for bits and pieces."

"Must be great fun. I'll bet you're a big help to the professor. You know, I'd love to go on one of those digs and help discover new artifacts."

"Well, a lot of adults take summer classes. It's the advanced students who get to go on these trips. Graduate students, mostly. But there are digs here in the States, too, and sometimes they use volunteers."

"I'll have to look into that." He nodded toward a plate on the next shelf. It stood on a small display stand. "Now, that's not a replica."

She reached for it. "No, that's something that belonged to my grandmother."

"Dresden china?"

"Why, yes." She turned it over and showed him the hallmark on the back.

"Beautiful."

"You're not an antique dealer, are you?" She eyed him suspiciously.

"No, no worries there. Although I do some work for an insurance company, and they insure collections. But my mother had a few pieces of Dresden, and I thought I recognized it. Not that pattern, though." He held his smile and forced himself not to look up at the shelf where he thought the item of most interest to Petra rested. "Thank you for showing me your treasures."

"Well, I hope you catch up with my husband sometime. You'd enjoy talking to him. He could tell you so much more than I can."

Joe nodded and let his eyes rove slowly over the shelves on the side wall that Petra had indicated. There were only a couple of items that he thought fit her vague description. He zeroed in on one that sat on a shelf slightly above his own eye level. Harwood was a tall man, he knew. That piece seemed the most likely. He pointed toward it.

"This is an odd vase. Or is it a pitcher?"

"Oh, that's a Toby jug."

"Something your husband found?"

"No, they're English, mostly. I believe his family had several of those. My in-laws were collectors. His stepmother made it her hobby after she married Rexford's father."

"He lost his own mother, did he?"

"When he was still in grade school. Very sad it was. Before I'd met him."

"That would have a big impact on a young man."

"Yes, I'm sure it did. His father struggled for several years, raising his son alone. But as I said, his father married again. And Rexford turned out a fine man. "

"I hope things are easier for his father now," Joe murmured.

"He's passed on."

"I'm sorry. He had a fancy for antiques, though?"

Mrs. Harwood nodded. "More Rex's stepmother. She's gone now, too. But she liked to bargain for antiques and poke around little shops. That jug is the last of her collection. The rest were all sold."

"May I?" Joe reached tentatively toward it.

"Let me." She stretched to lift it down tenderly and placed it in his hands. "It's very old."

Joe held the pitcher toward the light from the patio door and examined it. The jug was shaped like a fat little colonial man with a red jacket and brown knee breeches, holding a mug in one hand. The liquid in the jug would pour out one corner of his tricorn hat. Joe chuckled. "Such a merry little fellow."

"Yes, everyone loves them. They each have their own personality."

Joe's phone rang softly.

145

"Excuse me. I'll let you take this. I wouldn't want to drop it." He handed her the jug and turned toward the glass door as he took out his phone. "Hello?"

Petra whispered, "That's it."

Joe said briskly, "All right, thank you. I'll be there in a little while." He closed the connection and smiled at his hostess. "I'm afraid I have to go, but I've enjoyed our visit very much."

"Well, so have I, Mr. Tarleton. You may leave your card for my husband if you'd like. Perhaps you can come another time."

Joe mentally catalogued the business cards in his wallet. Private detective wouldn't do, but he had a few the insurance company had sent him with their company name and logo, for times when he represented them. He extracted one and handed it to her. "Thank you so much."

"You're in insurance?"

"Yes, I work for that company, but I'm not here to sell you or your husband anything. I'm sure you have adequate coverage for your fine home and collections."

He exited with as much aplomb as he could muster and drove slowly down the street. Instead of turning directly onto Acton, he went as far as the McDonald's and took a turn through their parking lot, then headed back to Petra's house. She was waiting for him with the garage door up, although darkness was falling.

"What took you so long?"

He smiled. "Sorry. The professor wasn't home, and I had to take some time to get his wife to trust me. And I didn't want to drive directly back here, in case she was watching."

They went into Petra's kitchen, and he took out his phone.

"You think that jug I was holding was it?"

She nodded. "As soon as you turned around with it in front of you, I knew. It was just like when she held it. The colors, the size. That had to be what the woman was holding when he attacked her."

"Want to see it up close? I managed to click a picture while she wasn't looking."

Petra took the phone and gazed at the screen. "Wow. He's kinda cute."

"And he has a pedigree. Tonight I'm going to do a little background check on Mr. Toby Jug."

Petra awoke in darkness. All was still. Too still. No birds, no crickets, no humming refrigerator. What had wakened her?

She heard a slight noise. Mason shifting his position?

No, Mason was gone. She'd left him with her sisters last weekend.

Her heart leaped into her throat, and she reached out for her night stand, touching nothing. Her pulse raced.

Easy, now. Take it slow.

She swished her hand through the air, then leaned farther to the side. Her fingers brushed the lamp. She clicked the switch, and light flooded the room. The boxes she'd filled with clothes and photo albums sat in the corner. Otherwise, the room looked the same as always.

Another noise, soft but identifiable, reached her ears. She grabbed her phone and pushed 911.

"What is your emergency?"

"Someone is in my house."

"Are you reporting a break-in?"

"Yes. I heard someone in the kitchen, and the front door just closed."

"I show your address as 133 Acton Street."

"That's right."

"An officer will be sent over. Please hold the line."

Petra swung her feet over the edge of the bed and snatched her robe off a chair. As she stood, a wave of nauseating scent struck her, and she clutched the phone. "I smell gas."

"Do you have a gas stove, ma'am?"

"Yes." As she spoke, Petra tore barefooted down the hallway, flipping every light switch she passed. She burst into the kitchen and slid to a stop in front of the range. The dial for the back left burner was turned to high, but no flame showed. She whipped the dial to off.

"A burner was on, but I shut it off."

"You'd better go outside, ma'am. You don't want to inhale too much of the gas."

Petra stared toward the front door. What if he was waiting outside to see if she emerged into the night? "I . . . I'm afraid to go out."

"Then open the windows. Do you have a kitchen fan you can turn on? Get some ventilation through there."

An hour later she locked the door of her hotel room with trembling hands. She sat down hard in a chair. Her phone stared up at her, daring her to pick it up.

God, help me.

She took it in her hand and clicked to Contacts. The sight of Joe's name comforted her, and she pushed Send.

"Tarleton!"

She smiled involuntarily at his grouchy, sleepy greeting. "I'm sorry to wake you . . ."

"Petra. What is it? Are you okay?"

"Someone broke into my house."

"When?"

"An hour or so ago. They made a noise, and I woke up. I was half asleep, and I thought it must be Mason at first, because if it was someone else moving around, he'd be barking."

"But Mason's up here." Joe's deep voice now had that reassuring tone that centered her whenever she heard it.

148

"Yes. I called the police, and then I smelled gas."

"Gas? Petra!"

"I think he tried to kill me." Tears gushed into her eyes and spilled down her cheeks.

"The police came?"

"Yes. They searched the house."

"Did they find anything? You said you had the locks changed."

Petra sobbed. "Yes, but that didn't stop him. He broke a window in the guest room. They think he came in there and went out the front door. It was unlocked when I got up."

She heard Joe sigh.

"You okay?" he asked.

"Yes. They wanted me to go to the hospital and get checked out, but I told them I didn't need to."

"I'd feel better if you did."

"An EMT looked me over, and the police officer brought me to a hotel." She brushed back a tear.

"Good."

"Joe, the cop said I probably left the burner on by mistake."

After a moment's silence, Joe said, "People do forget things like that, especially if they're stressed."

"No. I didn't turn the stove on after you left, and we'd have noticed if it was on when you were there."

"If you did . . . I suppose the flame could have gone out?"

"No. Joe, I heard him leave."

"Okay, okay."

Another silence clawed at her heart. She'd been foolish in thinking she would be safe because she had a new dead bolt. Even though she'd been afraid, she'd refused to give up her independence.

"You believe me, don't you?" she whispered. "About the gas?"

"Yes."

No hesitation there. She blew out a breath. "Thank you. If it hadn't been for the broken window, I don't think they'd have taken me seriously at all."

"I wish I could be there with you. Did you tell the police about the keys?"

"Yes, but the officer didn't seem to think it was important, since the locksmith was here yesterday."

Joe sighed. "Okay."

"I didn't mention Rex Harwood," Petra said. "I told them I missed my extra key ring and someone might have taken it. They weren't wild about the theory. They asked if I'd given out any other keys, and I told them about the boy who comes to mow the lawn and feed Mason when I'm gone. They're going to check with him tomorrow and see if he's lost the key. But I figured if I mentioned Rex again, I'd have some sort of harassment suit slapped on me."

"I'm so sorry. Do you want me to come down?"

She could hear the frustration and fatigue in his voice.

Yes! I want you here. I want you to keep me safe and tell me no one will hurt me. I want you to make him leave me alone.

She took a deep breath. "No. I'll be okay."

"Petra, you have a visitor."

Petra looked up in surprise from updating a patient's chart. Surely Joe hadn't come to Portland this morning. He'd called her again at 6:30, and she'd assured him that she was all right and headed for work. She peeked into the ER's waiting room. Several people sat in the chairs, their expressions varying from boredom to agony. A handsome man in a suit stood near the entrance, looking about with an alertness that shouted "cop."

Her pulse accelerated. *Now what?* She went back to the nurses' station and told her supervisor she would take her break.

150

"Miss Wilson?" the man said as she approached him.

"Yes. Would you care to step out into the hallway?"

"Thank you."

Outside the ER, he smiled at her. "I'm Detective Nick Wyatt."

She shook his hand, appraising him. Joe's age, but Nick looked younger with sun-bleached hair and a cowlick. Joe's friend; a man he trusted and turned to for help when he needed it. A very good cop, according to Joe, and a cop on her side now, unless last night's episode had swayed him.

"I'm pleased to meet you," she said. "Perhaps we could step over to the coffee shop."

"Good idea." As they walked down the hallway, Nick said, "Joe and I are working pretty closely on your case now."

"I'm glad to hear that."

"It must be very stressful for you."

"You've no idea."

They ordered coffee and sat in a corner out of the traffic pattern.

"I spoke with Joe this morning," Nick told her, "to update him on what I've been doing. He told me about the intruder at your house last night. Are you okay?"

"It shook me up pretty badly, but I'm all right."

Nick nodded. "I understand you didn't name any suspects."

"It didn't seem wise, in light of past events."

"But you think Rex Harwood came in and blew out the pilot light on the stove and turned the gas on."

"Well . . . someone poisoned my dog last week. After that, I realized my key ring was gone. I do think Harwood may have tried the lock and then broken the spare room window. And I don't know of anyone else who would want to harm me."

Nick held her gaze for a long moment. "I hope we can clear this up for you. All of it. I admit I was skeptical when Joe first contacted me about your case, but it's beginning to make sense."

"I appreciate that."

"And Joe's told you about the car that was left at the airport?" he asked.

"Yes. Did you find the owner?"

"Unfortunately, no. It's registered to a woman living outside Halifax, Nova Scotia, and she seems to be missing."

"That's a shame."

"Yes. She's a widow, living alone. The police in Halifax have contacted her children, friends and neighbors, but no one seems to have known she was going to Portland that day." Nick sipped his coffee.

"Could the car have been stolen in Nova Scotia and driven down here?"

"I don't think so, but we're considering all options. I believe she did come to Portland."

"Do you know how long she was in town?" Petra asked.

"Good question. I checked with the ferry terminal. This car came over on the catamaran ferry from Yarmouth, Nova Scotia, on May sixteenth. We're checking hotels to see if we find that the owner stayed at one of them overnight. And you saw what you saw on the seventeenth."

"That's right. Early evening."

Nick nodded. "The car was parked at the airport the morning of the eighteenth. The question is, did Mrs. Foster leave it there, or did someone else?"

"Mrs. Foster? That's the owner?"

"Yes, sorry. Harriet Foster. As you can imagine, the police and the airport management want to find her as soon as possible. So far, we've established that she did not hold a reservation on any plane leaving Portland on the eighteenth."

"And someone saw her car on Rex Harwood's street the night of the seventeenth."

Nick smiled. "Yes. Joe picked up on that. I might have. Then again, I might not. He's got a special kind of brain, Joe has."

And a special kind of heart, she thought.

"Mr. Wyatt—"

"Please call me Nick." He drew back and reached for his coffee.

"I suppose Joe told you about his little stunt—going over to talk to Mrs. Harwood."

"Oh, yes, and I chewed him out for it. He could blow my investigation if he's not careful."

"I was surprised she let him in," Petra admitted.

"Well, Joe's got charm oozing out his ears."

"Hasn't he?" They both laughed.

"How can you be sure, from such a distance, that the jug Joe saw is the same item the woman was holding when she was strangled?"

Petra drew in a deep breath. "I wasn't certain at first. But when Joe held it, the colors were the same as my memory of it. I see that picture every night in my dreams, vividly. Her face, mostly. But the thing she held . . . it's there, too. She was holding it against her chest and screaming at Rex. And when she fell to the floor, he . . . he picked it up so gently . . ." She flexed her shoulders. "His wife handled it with the same reverence last night. When Joe showed me the photo he took, I was absolutely sure. No question."

Nick nodded slowly. "All right. Joe is doing some research on that particular type of ceramics, and he'll share the information with me. My job today is to try to establish where Mrs. Foster stayed in Portland, and what her connection is to Rex Harwood."

"Don't they have cameras at the airport?" Petra asked. "They might have footage of whoever drove the car there. And he must have called a taxi to take him somewhere afterward."

"We're on it," Nick said. "They don't have cameras on that part of the parking lot. But we do have an officer working the taxi angle. Of course, it's been more than two weeks now. A passenger would have to stand out for some reason in a cab driver's mind for him to remember it so long, and to be able to fix the date. So that's a long shot, but we are checking." He glanced at his watch. "Well, I'd better get going. Best case scenario, we'll find a cab driver who recalls picking Mrs. Foster up at the airport that night."

"Worst case scenario, some driver remembers picking Rex up?"

Nick shook his head. "Worst case scenario is nothing. Nobody saw a thing."

Chapter thirteen

Joe entered his office yawning on Wednesday morning. He'd been up half the night working at the computer. A case this absorbing rarely came his way. His briefcase held the reams of information he'd gathered about Rex Harwood, the Cat ferry, Portland International Airport, and Toby jugs. And Petra. Nick had emailed him a preliminary report on her. *Just thought you'd like to know my background check on Miss Wilson is clean so far,* his note had read. *No solid clues as to the identity of the intruder at her house, though. An officer will be at her house this morning while workmen fix the broken window.*

Joe tamped down his initial anger when he read that Nick had done a background check on Petra. *Just doing his job.* Joe had purposely held back from digging too deeply into Petra's past. He wanted to let her unveil her history to him, so he could learn it the same way he was learning her personality. He loved her insistence on truth, her determination to learn what lay behind the awful scene she'd witnessed. Joe had a feeling the same intensity wove into other areas of her life, yet he'd seen an occasional touch of lightness.

Finding Petra in the middle of an intriguing case was the ultimate bonus. He'd begun to think they were well matched. For a long time, he'd shied away from entering a permanent relationship. He didn't want to get into something that turned bad. His parents' breakup had taught him one thing well:

caution. But with Petra . . . Lately he found himself looking more closely at Nick and Robin's marriage. He didn't doubt they loved each other, though they sometimes disagreed vigorously. And they'd been together fifteen years. Maybe it wasn't impossible to have a lifelong, happy marriage.

I wonder if Petra only seems ideal for me because she needs my help and protection. That was a recurring thought that sobered him. Would the mutual attraction fade once the case was solved? Joe sat down at his desk and bowed his head for a moment. *Lord, help me to see things clearly, and help us to find the truth about Rex Harwood.* He turned on the computer and opened his briefcase.

After several hours of research, his stomach growled. He sat back and sorted the papers he'd printed out during this session. By now he considered himself somewhat of an expert on Toby jugs. The one in Harwood's house must be worth somewhere in the neighborhood of $12,000, if he was any judge of its condition and current prices.

He picked up his telephone receiver and dialed the number for the gift shop next door. As it rang, he wished he'd stopped by instead, on his way out for lunch. Keilah's bright voice answered.

"You Shouldn't Have."

Joe smiled. "Yeah, yeah, I know I shouldn't have. Any messages for me?"

"None this morning, which is rather remarkable, don't you think?"

"I sure do. But it's okay. I've got plenty of work right now." He hung up wishing Petra would tell her sisters that he was working for her and why. It made things awkward sometimes. He and Keilah had developed a bantering rapport, and a couple of times he'd had to catch himself from saying something that would make her curious. Bethany seemed quieter and more pensive, but then, she was older, and she'd been widowed. Joe found he could enjoy a serious conversation with Bethany, and she, too, could enter into Keilah's silliness on occasion. Still, he found himself thinking of Keilah as a . . . *Yeah,* he acknowledged inwardly, *I can see her as a younger sister.*

He liked that. The feeling of being a sibling in a large family agreed with him. If things continued to progress with him and Petra . . .

Suddenly, he wanted to hear her voice. He dialed her cell phone number. She wouldn't answer; she was probably at the hospital and had the phone stashed in her locker. But just hearing her speak on her voice mail would give him a fix.

"Joe?"

Her voice surprised him, and his heart lurched.

"Yeah. Aren't you working?"

"One of the other nurses and I are on our lunch hour, and we decided to get out of the hospital for a change."

He was smiling, although she couldn't see him. Probably a goofy smile. "I just wanted to see how you were doing."

"Fine. Nick Wyatt stopped by this morning."

"What did you think of him?"

"I like him," she said. "I did get the feeling he was sizing me up."

"He believes you now. The car convinced him, so don't worry about that."

"Mm. Anything new?"

"I'm learning all I can about certain antiques, if you get my drift. Listen, why don't you ask Nick to tell your boss you have to leave early? Come up here and get away from . . . you know who."

"I . . . can't talk about this now, Joe."

He sighed. "Okay. I'll let you go, but we'll talk again soon."

"Thanks."

He hated to hang up, but he knew he could best serve her by putting something in his stomach and getting back to work.

And he did have another case he needed to put some time in on today.

The other matter sent him to Augusta after lunch, and he stopped at the county courthouse for some records. While he was at it, he decided to ask for a copy of Rex Harwood's father's will. The clerk kept him waiting fifteen minutes while she searched, but she came up dry.

"I'm sorry," she told him. "We don't have a record of his will being probated in Kennebec County. If he died in another county, or in another state, we wouldn't have it here."

Joe sighed. "Why aren't all of the records standardized? You should be able to check statewide records instantly with that computer."

She gave him a rather sour smile. "We're working on it, sir, but the backlog is huge."

Joe got a burger and two cups of coffee. He picked up a paper to read while he ate. A sudden thought sent him to the classifieds in the back of the paper. Sure enough, a couple of estate auctions were advertised for the coming weekend. One of the auctioneers was an antique dealer well known in the area. Joe drove back up the interstate past Waterville and got off at the next town. At the auction hall, he parked in the empty lot and got out, but the door was locked. The action on a Wednesday afternoon seemed to be across the lot at the rambling antique shop.

He entered and sauntered through the rooms, hands in his pockets. Wouldn't want to break a five-hundred-dollar vase. Joe had never seen so much old stuff. One set of shelves held hundreds of glass insulators—the kind they used to use on telephone poles when he was a kid. One section was filled with old farm implements. Then furniture. Bottles. Dishes.

He wandered around the dish section but didn't spot any Toby jugs. He did find a couple of newer "character jugs" that he'd learned were distant cousins to Toby.

He eventually wandered back toward the door. A man stood behind the counter, ringing up a purchase for a middle-aged couple.

"Thanks very much. Come again." The man smiled and turned his attention to Joe. "May I help you, sir?"

Joe pulled out one of his private investigator business cards.

"Yes, I'm interested in Toby jugs."

"Ah. Wonderful collectibles, but the genuine ones are becoming rare."

Joe nodded. "So I've learned. Have you seen any in this neck of woods lately?"

"I had one a year or two back, but I don't see them often." The man shook his head.

"They say they might have gotten the name from a Shakespearean character," Joe noted. "Sir Toby Belch."

The man grinned. "That's appropriate."

"Yeah, well, it's probably not true." Joe shrugged.

"I recall a big collection being sold—oh, three or four years ago," the man said. "But I didn't handle them. The sale was at Gillespie's in Portland. I attended."

"Could you write down the name of the dealer for me?"

"Sure. I've got his phone number here, too. Calvin Gillespie. Does a lot of high-end auctions in southern Maine. I might still have the catalog from that sale on file." He disappeared into an alcove, and Joe waited. A minute later the man reappeared and slipped a magazine-sized brochure into his hand. "There you go. You can take that if you like."

"Thanks very much." Another customer was waiting behind him, so Joe nodded and left the shop. He realized it was nearly suppertime and drove back to his office, arriving just as Bethany and Keilah locked up their store.

"Joe, would you like to come out to the house for supper?" Bethany called.

Her offer tempted him, but Joe wanted to stay on Petra's case, so he declined. Inside the office, he went straight to his computer. There were only half a dozen daily newspapers in Maine. He went after their archived obituaries methodically. In his initial investigation of Rex's parents, he'd found Anne Fuller Harwood's obituary easily, in the Augusta paper, but not Ernest Harwood's. Time to dig deeper. Bangor, Lewiston, Portland . . .

An hour later he called out for pizza and kept at it. Just as the delivery boy arrived, he hit pay dirt with the *Portland Press Herald*. Ernest Harwood had died in Biddeford three years ago. Joe paid for the pizza and went back to the computer to print the obituary, scanning it on the screen while he waited. Survived by his son, Rexford, three stepchildren, and several grandchildren. Joe leaned back in his chair and squinted at the screen. Very interesting.

Petra drove as quickly as traffic would allow to the Henry Wadsworth Longfellow House on Thursday. After today, only one more day of work. She pulled onto a side street, as parking in front of the Longfellow House and Maine Historical Society buildings was always iffy. After locking her car, she hurried to the little garden at the side of the old brick home. Joe was waiting for her, wandering about the small park and admiring the plants.

"Good afternoon!" She hurried to meet him and noticed several takeout food containers on a bench.

"Hi." He stooped to kiss her cheek lightly. "Chinese okay?"

"Terrific. Is everything all right?"

"Yeah. I'm sorry I called you so early this morning, but I wanted to be sure to catch you before you left for work."

"I was surprised you were coming down here again so soon."

"Well, you know—business."

Petra wondered how large his bill for expenses would be. After all, she was giving up her secure income after next week. "Do you need gas money?"

"Oh, don't worry about the expenses."

That was a relief, but it raised new questions. Maybe her case wasn't generating new leads anymore. "Is this trip for another client?"

"Well, no, but . . ." His voice dropped to deep and confidential, and he took her hand in his. "I've got a personal stake in this now, Petra."

Warmth spread over her. He cared about her on a deeper level, and she had to admit she was liking that more and more.

"I can't believe this place is vacant." Joe pushed aside the food containers, and they sat down on the bench. "I was afraid a busload of kids would be taking the tour."

She smiled. "God arranged it for us, I guess."

He asked a blessing on the food and opened one of the boxes. "Crab Rangoon?"

"I love it." She took a napkin and the hot, delicious Chinese food. Joe handed her a bottle of diet cola that was still cold. She asked, "So, you've had a breakthrough?"

"Not exactly. But I learned that a private collection of Toby jugs was sold at a large auction house in Portland a few years ago. I came down to talk to the auctioneer this afternoon."

"You think they were the Harwood family's antiques?"

"I don't know, but Mrs. Harwood did say her mother-in-law had a large collection and they'd been sold. The timing of the sale is right—a few months after Rex's father died. His stepmother predeceased her husband."

Petra tried to follow that and pictured a family tree chart in her mind. "So, his mother died when Rex was a kid, and his father got married again, and the new stepmother liked antiques. . ."

"Right. I found out her first husband was a doctor, but they divorced. She seems to have had money of her own when she married Ernest Harwood."

"Let me know how it goes."

"I will. I also learned Rex had two stepbrothers and a stepsister."

"What happened to them?"

"Well, one of the brothers is retired from the Navy, living in California. The other one died of a heart attack five years ago."

Petra opened another container and discovered beef and broccoli. "And the step-sister?" She reached for a set of plastic silverware.

"Get this. Back in the 1960s she married Isaac Foster, a businessman from Nova Scotia."

Petra paused and stared at him. "The Nova Scotia connection!"

"I think so."

"Did you tell Nick?"

"Yes. He's meeting me here. When you go back to work, he's going to go with me to the auction house. He said he'd call ahead for an appointment with the owner."

"Great." She smiled. "Joe, we're going to solve this case."

"I sure hope so." He took her hand for a moment and squeezed it. "You gave me a scare the other night. Are you sure you're all right?"

"Yes."

"I wish you'd stay at the hotel and—"

She held up a hand. "You know what? I agree."

He stared at her. "Really?"

"Yes. After last night, I don't want to stay at my house alone again. But it's only for one night. I talked to my supervisor at work, and I have a week's vacation left. She wasn't happy about it, but she agrees my contract says I can take it next week. That means tomorrow's my last day at the hospital."

"Excellent."

She frowned and bent her head to one side. "It's not ideal. I feel guilty because I know they're short-staffed in the ER. But things are getting so creepy, I just don't want to stay another week. So after my shift tomorrow, I'm going to Waterville. The real estate agent will deal with the house."

"That's great. I know you're not doing it for me, but thank you."

"I'll be so glad when all of this is over. I didn't want to take this whole mess with me to Bethany and Keilah."

Joe set his tray down. "Why haven't you told them?"

"I didn't want them to worry."

He frowned. "I'm not sure I buy that."

"What?" His expression hurt her as much as his words.

"You know they're sensible women. They'd do anything they could to help you. And I think it would be a relief to you if you could talk to them about it."

Petra studied his serious face. His square chin and deep brown eyes had become dear to her, and she could no longer disregard anything he said.

"Maybe . . ." The thought that came to her was hard to accept, but it wouldn't go away. "Maybe it's pride."

Joe's lips flattened as he considered that. "Think so?"

Petra gazed at the stone wall bordering the garden. "From the start I was afraid they wouldn't believe me. What if they'd told me I didn't know what I was talking about?" She looked at him with a shrug. "The police told me that. It was too much like . . . like the way I felt when Danny yelled at me and told me how stupid I was."

"Danny?"

"My . . . fiancé. You know."

He nodded. "But we have proof now. The car was there, on Harwood's street. That's one solid fact we have. But even

163

without any evidence, Bethany and Keilah would have believed you."

She looked down at her food container. "Probably. I ... hadn't been around them much for years until they moved to Waterville. They'd both lived in other states for a long time. I wasn't sure how they'd react to a lot of things. I felt like a stranger to them. But once I started seeing more of them, that went away. I was a sister again, and I could see that they loved me, no matter what. You know how it is when you're a kid and you think your siblings hate you? But when you grow up, you know that's silly, and . . ."

Joe shook his head, and his eyes held a look of incomprehension. Petra stopped. How could you express the feeling of sisterhood to an only child—an only son at that?

Joe's chin lifted, and he smiled as he looked along the narrow garden toward the street. She followed his gaze. Nick Wyatt came down the steps that led up to street level.

"Hey, Joseph!" He nodded at Petra. "Nice to see you again, Miss Wilson."

She smiled and looked to Joe for a cue.

Joe stood and reached to shake Nick's hand. "Did you eat?"

"Yeah, I'm all set, thanks."

"You got anything new?" Joe asked.

Nick nodded. "I think we're on our way, thanks to the lead you gave me this morning." He looked at Petra and included them both in his announcement. "This is breaking. We confirmed what you suspected, Joe. The owner of the car abandoned at the airport was Rex Harwood's stepsister, Harriet Foster."

Joe exhaled heavily. "What do you know? And nobody's seen her since her trip to Portland."

"That's right. Seems she didn't tell anyone in Nova Scotia that she was coming."

"I wonder if the professor knew," Joe mused.

164

"I'm thinking about interviewing Mrs. Harwood again." Nick and Joe sat down. "But first we'll go see that auctioneer you told me about."

"Why don't you just pick Rex up and ask him about his stepsister?" Petra asked.

Nick bobbed his head and smiled. "I want a little more evidence first. Enough so we can hold him. I don't want to have to go after him twice."

"Yeah, we want an ironclad case." Joe started closing up the food containers. "Think you can get a match on that hair?"

"The Halifax police are sending us some of Mrs. Foster's hair that her family let them take from her hairbrush. We should have it today. It will take a while to do DNA, but they may be able to match the two hair samples fairly conclusively. And I talked to the stepbrother in California."

Petra glanced at her watch. "Quick. I need to get back to work. What did he say?"

Nick shrugged. "Said Rex was a little twerp, and he couldn't stand him. He admitted he and his brother used to pick on him a lot. He never got along with the stepfather—that's Ernest Harwood, Rex's father. As soon as Robert turned seventeen, he got his mother to sign for him so he could join the navy."

"Has he kept in contact with Rex's side of the family?" Joe asked.

"Nope. I guess the sister has somewhat. Rex notified Harriet when his father died, and she came over for Ernest Harwood's funeral. Robert—that's the older brother—said as far as he knew, that was the last time Harriet saw Rex. He opted not to attend the funeral, since his mother was already dead and he had no use for Ernest or Rex."

"Did you tell him his sister is missing now?" Petra asked. She felt sorry for Nick, having that job.

"Yeah. He asked us to let him know as soon as we find out anything. He'll check into flights, but I told him it was early to come back here. When we've got something solid . . ."

"I hope that's soon." Petra stood and picked up her purse. "Thanks for keeping me in the loop, guys."

Joe jumped up. "I'll walk you to your car."

"Pretty girl," Nick said as they watched Petra drive away. "Is she going to the Sox game with us?"

Joe grinned. "I forgot to ask her."

"There's time." Nick clapped him on the shoulder. "Come on, let's get out of here."

They decided to ride together to the auction hall, which was ten miles away. Joe snagged his briefcase from his own car and climbed into Nick's unmarked cruiser.

"You know, I got a copy of Ernest Harwood's will this morning. Stopped at the Cumberland County courthouse before I met Petra for lunch."

"And?" Nick asked.

"He left everything to Rex."

"Nothing to the stepkids?"

Joe shook his head. "Nope. So that makes me wonder . . ."

Nick eyed him critically and pulled out into traffic. "Yeah?"

"I think we should take a look at Mrs. Harwood's will. Rex's stepmother, I mean. She had money and she bought antiques. Don't you think she'd have left something to her own children? Her husband left his estate to his own son, not her kids. She may have done the same."

Nick frowned. "You think they had a pre-nup?"

Joe thought about that. "Possibly. Or they could have made a verbal agreement—my money goes to my kids, yours goes to your son."

"But Rex had the Toby jug that belonged to her." Nick hit the brake as the light ahead of them turned red.

"My point exactly. His stepsister came over from Halifax unannounced, and the two of them wound up arguing over an antique that had belonged to her mother. Mrs. Harwood told me that piece had belonged to her mother-in-law—Rex's stepmother."

"Worth looking into."

They arrived at the auction hall half an hour later, after fighting noon-hour traffic all the way. Joe banished all thoughts of the last night he served as a patrolman in Portland, though they battered at the edges of his mind as they crawled through the streets he'd worked with Nick.

Before they entered the building, Joe consulted the copied obituary in his briefcase and waited for Nick to make a call to his detective sergeant, requesting that an officer be sent to the courthouse for a copy of Laura Harwood's will.

"You're joking," Nick said into his phone. His face went all stiff and shocked. Joe stepped closer, into Nick's line of vision. "All right, thanks, Sarge." Nick put his phone away and took a deep breath. "Things are happening fast, Joe, my man."

"What is it?"

"A body."

Chapter fourteen

Joe's adrenaline surged. "Where did they find the body?"

"Durham," Nick replied. "Just north of Freeport. A woman. Middle-aged, they think. Off the road a little ways in the woods, barely covered with dirt."

"What was she wearing?"

"Didn't say."

"Call back and ask him."

Nick looked doubtful. "I don't think the sergeant has the details yet. Come on. We'll talk to this auction guy, then I'll touch base with the State Police. It may not be our victim."

Joe ground his teeth and followed Nick inside. The hall and its owner were more sophisticated than the ones Joe had visited farther north. A woman greeted them as they entered and led them to an office near the front of the building. Joe got a glimpse into the large, open room where the auctions were held and estimated two hundred chairs filled it.

Nick made the introductions, blurring the lines of Joe's involvement, as he showed the man his badge. "Hi, I'm detective Nick Wyatt with the Portland P.D., and this is detective Joe Tarleton."

Joe didn't enlighten anyone as to his unofficial status. Calvin Gillespie rose to shake hands. Joe judged him to be in his fifties, with graying hair and glasses. His neat gray slacks and light blue dress shirt gave him a more professional air than most antique dealers. Apparently he ran his business from this crowded but well-organized room.

"Sir, we're here about a sale you conducted three years ago," Nick said.

Joe edged forward and slid the catalog with a colorful cover photo of a Toby jug onto the man's desk.

"Oh, the Tobys?" Gillespie picked up the catalog and nodded. "That was a good sale."

"How much did it bring?" Nick asked.

"I'd have to look up the records to be sure. Close to two hundred thousand, I think."

"And who was the seller?"

Gillespie hesitated. "I'm bound to keep that information confidential."

"This is part of a murder investigation," Nick said.

"Well, I . . . suppose you can get a warrant."

"We can if we have to." Nick eyed him carefully. "You can speed things up a bit by cooperating here, sir."

Gillespie sighed and went to a file cabinet. "Here." He pulled out a manila folder and plunked it in Nick's hand. Nick opened it, and Joe read over his shoulder.

"That's our guy," Joe said softly.

Nick nodded. "Could you please ask your secretary to make a copy of this folder for the police, sir?"

"Sure." The auctioneer took the folder.

"The catalog says there were about thirty pieces in the collection of Toby jugs," Joe said.

Gillespie nodded. "All pristine. You know, in this business, condition is everything. And all of those were great pieces." He glanced inside the folder. "One hundred eighty-five thousand dollars gross. That was top dollar. Selling it as a collection enhanced the price."

"You're saying you got more for the collection than you would have separately?" Nick asked.

"Yes, I believe so. That happens sometimes, especially when the seller has handpicked the items over a period of time to complement each other. And good Toby jugs are getting scarce." Gillespie walked to the door and said to the secretary, "Andrea, would you please make a copy of everything in this folder for the gentlemen? Not the catalog. They have that."

Joe went outside and paced the parking lot while he waited for Nick to get the copies and finish up with Gillespie. At last Nick came out, handed him the sheaf of papers and got behind the wheel. As his friend drove, Joe skimmed the information and then put the papers in his briefcase. He closed the latches just as Nick pulled into the parking garage at the police station.

"Why don't you come inside with me?" Nick asked.

"You sure?"

Nick shrugged. "The sarge knows you're an alumnus of this place and that we're breaking a murder case largely thanks to you. No problem."

"Okay." Even so, Joe's adrenaline kicked up a notch as they entered the police station. He hadn't been inside since the day he turned in his badge. Officers greeted Nick every few steps, but Joe didn't recognize any of them.

Nick took him directly to the detectives' area and nodded toward a chair facing his desk. Joe sat down, still looking around uneasily. He had once aspired to earning the rank of detective in this department. From outside, he'd been able to congratulate Nick and feel satisfaction and a bit of pride in his former partner. Now he wondered if he'd been rash to quit when he did. He could have a desk across the aisle from Nick and wear the badge with the confidence the city's authority gave.

A uniformed officer approached Nick and handed him a large envelope. Nick opened it. "Oh, good. Here's the will you wanted." He handed it to Joe.

Joe was surprised and pleased that Nick let him take the first look at it. He pulled out the document and scanned it.

171

Vindication and apprehension struggled in his heart as he made sense of the legalese. He glanced up and saw that Nick had leaned back, waiting for him to share anything pertinent to the case.

"Laura Harwood left ten thousand dollars to each of her two sons, and all of her dishes to her daughter, Harriet Foster."

"Dishes." Nick frowned so hard the front lock of his blond hair covered his sandy eyebrows. "Are those Toby jugs considered dishes?"

"You betcha." Joe continued to read silently, more and more certain that he had found the key to the murder. "Anything else left in her estate went to her husband. This is your motive."

"Rex had already got the money from the auction before he murdered the sister."

"Yes, he sold the collection that was rightfully Harriet's. She wanted it, and he killed her so she wouldn't turn him in for stealing it."

"Maybe." Nick relaxed, limp, in his padded chair, staring off toward the door of the break room. Joe had seen the skeptical look on his face hundreds of times before.

"Nicky, you know people have killed for a lot less."

The phone on the desk rang, and Nick leaned forward to grab the receiver.

"Detective Wyatt. Yes. Uh-huh." He scribbled notes on a scrap of paper. "Got it." He hung up and met Joe's inquiring gaze straight on. "The body they found in Durham."

Joe's pulse quickened. "Yeah?"

"It matches the description Petra gave of the woman Harwood strangled. Black slacks and knit top. Red scarf."

Petra strode across the parking lot toward her car, glad once again to be leaving work in full daylight. She wondered how much progress Joe and Nick had made. With both of them

172

actively pursuing the truth, the case would soon be solved. Rex Harwood would be locked up, and she could breathe easily once more.

She hit the remote button to unlock her door and slipped into the driver's seat. The car was warm inside, but not stifling. The sun dipped westward, and the heat of the day was past. After starting the engine, she turned the fan on low.

She edged out of the lot into traffic, planning to stop at home for supper and her overnight bag, then drive to her hotel before dark.

The hairs on the back of her neck tickled, and she stiffened. A sound? No, a sense of movement behind her. She looked at the rearview mirror but saw nothing. She glanced over her shoulder and almost ran off the road. On the floor in the backseat, she saw legs and a man's brown leather shoe. She stomped on the brake, her heart lurching, and felt movement against the back of the seat as she looked forward to avoid running into anyone.

Behind her, a deep voice said, "Keep driving."

Nick and Joe sat in the unmarked car watching Rex Harwood's driveway. The warrant for Rex's arrest stuck out of Nick's breast pocket, and half a dozen officers kept their posts, concealed around the neighborhood. A female patrol officer was in the house with Mrs. Harwood, explaining the situation to her and making sure she did nothing to notify the professor of his impending arrest.

Joe looked at his watch for the twelfth time. "He should be here by now. It's five-thirty." He raised his binoculars and peered across the yard of the Harwoods' next-door neighbor. Through the foliage he could see just a bit of Acton Street and had been watching for Petra's red Avalon to glide into her driveway.

"Maybe he had to run an errand." Nick tapped the steering wheel with his thumbs. His cell phone rang, and he fished it from his pocket. "Detective Wyatt." His chin jerked up, and Joe instantly came alert. "Yes, ma'am, I remember. Yes, ma'am. And when did this happen?"

When he hung up, he turned to Joe, his face betraying his chagrin.

"Who was it?" Joe asked.

"That Eileen McAdams, down the street. The whiz kid's mother."

Joe nodded. "You told her to call you if she had anything. What's up?"

Nick looked away and winced. "She had a chat with Mrs. Harwood this afternoon."

"Oh, boy."

"They talked about Eileen's kids and the Harwoods' grandchildren and lilac bushes and detectives asking about cars from Nova Scotia."

"Just what we need."

"Yeah. If Mrs. H. put two and two together and asked her husband if anyone from Nova Scotia came around while she was visiting her sister in Millinocket last month . . ."

Joe nodded. "And right about then Rex recalled he had to run over to his office on campus this afternoon."

"His wife said he left two hours ago." Nick pounded his fist on the wheel.

"Call the men you sent over to the university."

Nick called and got a quick reply, which he relayed to Joe. "They're still watching the doors of the building, but they haven't spotted his SUV anywhere nearby."

"He ran." The certainty implanted itself deep in Joe's heart. "The discovery of the body went out on the early news. He probably listened to it on the radio after his wife tipped him off. He could be halfway to Quebec by now."

Nick reached for his radio transmitter. "I'll put out a bulletin for his vehicle on the interstate, north and south."

"You may be too late." Joe pulled out his phone and punched the speed dial for Petra. It rang twice and kicked to her voice mail. He inhaled slowly, willing his blood pressure not to skyrocket.

Nick paused with the microphone next to his mouth. "What's the matter?"

"Petra. She should be home by now, too."

"You want to check on her?"

Joe opened the car door. "I'll walk over there. Pick me up if you're leaving."

He bounded through the neighbors' unfenced yard and hopped over a low hedge onto the lawn next to Petra's. A short jog put him on the sidewalk paralleling Acton Street. He hurried to her driveway. No one answered the doorbell or his resonant pounding on the door panels. He turned away. An elderly woman stood on the sidewalk watching him. Her miniature dog—some kind of terrier, Joe guessed—let out several frantic yips.

"Hello," Joe said.

"Are you looking for someone?" the white-haired woman asked. She looked fragile enough to blow away in a good gale off the harbor.

"Petra Wilson," Joe told her.

The woman nodded. "I don't believe she's home yet."

"Thank you."

"She's moving, you know."

Joe had started to turn away, but he looked back at her. "Yes, I do know. Are you a friend of Miss Wilson?"

"Yes, and I'll miss her. Very sudden, this moving to Waterville." The old woman shook her head.

"Well, thanks again." Joe dashed back the way he'd come and slid into the passenger seat of Nick's car panting.

"Not home. I don't like this."

175

"I'm going over to the campus and see if we can find Harwood's vehicle. I'll leave two patrolmen here." Nick started the engine.

Joe called directory assistance, requested that the operator connect him to Maine Medical Center, and then asked for the nurses' station in the ER.

"Here," he told Nick a moment later, thrusting the phone at him. "They won't talk to me. Tell her you're a cop."

Nick pulled to the side of the street and put his flashers on, then spoke with the supervisor. A moment later he handed Joe back his phone. "Petra left an hour ago."

The air in the car was suddenly stifling. Joe felt sweat beading on his forehead. "Take me to my car."

"It's too far out of the way. We'll just go to the hospital."

Joe exhaled and wiped his brow with his sleeve. "Thanks."

Neither of them spoke until they rolled into the employees' parking lot. Joe zeroed in on one red car after another, but none of them was right.

"Maybe she had to park in the visitors' lot today," Nick said, easing the car along slowly.

"She was going to stay at a hotel tonight, but she told me she'd go home first to get some things." Joe had the sick, smothery feeling again. His stomach churned. "Hold it!"

Nick braked. "What?"

Joe pointed to a black SUV. "It's Harwood's vehicle. His plate number was in the police report when Petra first reported the murder. The patrolmen searched it in his garage."

"You sure that's it?"

"Positive."

"You . . . want me to get on 95?" Petra's voice shook, and she hated that. For years she had hidden her fears and regrets successfully. *Lord, make me strong now, when I really need it!*

"No!" She flinched at his sharp voice. "Just keep going straight for a while. We'll drive back roads. It will take longer, but there's no sense putting ourselves out there where people might start looking for you."

She followed his instructions to the letter, but even so, he seemed to enjoy touching the muzzle of his pistol to the back of her neck now and then. Funny, she'd always thought a gun barrel would feel cold against the skin. Evidently he'd hidden in the hot car long enough for the metal to warm.

Her lower lip twitched and she bit it. Berating herself for her stupidity did no good. She'd been so worried about securing her house and making sure he didn't enter it again that she'd given little thought to her car. But now that the case was breaking, she supposed he'd decided he had to get rid of the one witness, whatever it took.

She looked at the console and swallowed hard. "I'll need gas if we're going far."

He leaned forward, and she felt his face close beside her right cheek. She arched her spine away from him.

"You've got enough for a while," he snarled. "We'll find a place later, when we get out of town."

She continued driving west on Route 25, into a residential area. When he sat back a little, she could tell. His body heat no longer reached her. She tried to picture a map of the area west of Portland without success. Where was the auction hall Nick and Joe were visiting? She had an idea it was north of the city. But they were probably done there. Was Joe's car sitting in her driveway? Was he pacing the front yard right now, waiting for her? In her purse on the seat beside her lay her phone. How much of a chance would she have to reach it and dial for help without her abductor realizing what she was doing?

The hard metal touched her neck again, and she knew the answer. No chance at all.

Chapter fifteen

Nick threw his transmission into park. "Okay, breathe, Joe. I'm going to call some backup. Then we'll go into the ER and talk to her co-workers and see if anyone knows where she was parked. Someone coming on duty may have seen her get in her car."

Joe wanted to hit something. No, not something. Someone. Rex Harwood, to be precise. "Put out an alert for Petra's car."

"License plate?"

Joe put his fingers to the bridge of his nose and closed his eyes. He'd followed her home twice. Why couldn't he picture it?

"Not a vanity plate, I take it," Nick said.

Joe sighed. "It had a 6 in it." He felt stupid. How many times had he mentally flogged a witness for not being able to give an accurate description of a vehicle or a suspect? He prided himself on his memory for detail. Now, if Nick had asked him for the particulars of Petra's appearance, he'd have had it down to the precise angle of her bangs and the length of her eyelashes.

"Where's the whiz kid when you need him, eh?" Nick smiled. "Don't worry. The computer will find it for us."

"Right. Harwood stole her extra car keys when he broke into her house to poison the dog."

"She told me yesterday. You think he poisoned the dog to get rid of her alarm system?"

"I do. He intended to kill the mutt. And when he fiddled with Petra's gas stove, he intended to kill *her*. That didn't work, so he's taking a more direct approach."

Nick nodded grimly and reached for his radio transmitter. As he made the calls, Joe fought back his fear and tried to think. No sense dwelling now on all the things he should have done. He stared out over the acres of cars in the parking lot. Where would Rex Harwood take his next victim?

"I'm having his vehicle impounded," Nick said a minute later. "So now what?"

"He dumped Harriet's body in the woods."

Nick eyed him for a moment, then asked softly, "You think he'll do the same to Petra?"

"I don't know. Not in the same spot, that's for sure. He knows Harriet's been found, and he'll stay clear of there."

"Right," Nick said. "But he left Harriet's car at the airport."

Joe sat up and stared at him. "You don't think he'd do that again?"

Nick shrugged. "Doubt it. Still, it worked once." He turned on his blue lights and drove toward the international airport, at the same time speaking into his radio for backup.

Joe sat still, trying to think. Harwood was too smart to leave Petra's car the same place he'd left Harriet Foster's. But he couldn't come up with a better place to look.

A few minutes later they rolled up to the small booth where clerks took money and tickets from the patrons who parked in the airport's parking garage and outdoor short-term lots. Joe and Nick jumped out of the car and walked over to the building. An officer who drew duty at the airport as his regular beat met them at the door where the clerks entered for their shifts.

Nick greeted him and held up his badge. "I'm Detective Wyatt."

The patrolman nodded at him and Joe. "I've spoken to the parking lot manager, so he knows what's up. We'll distribute the license tag number and description of the vehicle to all the security personnel we can muster and see if the car's here."

"Great," Nick told him. "You should have at least four more uniforms arriving to help you."

"In that case, we should be able to cover this area and the long-term lots in less than an hour. Red Toyota Avalon. Should be easy to spot if it's here."

"What would be the easiest place to leave a car?" Nick asked.

The patrolman's eyes narrowed. "I'd have said right out here until yesterday, but since we found a suspicious car and the owner's missing, we've had security checking out any short-term parking tickets issued and not turned in within six hours."

"Well, this one wouldn't have been here that long yet," Nick said.

He and Joe opted to cover a section of the lot farthest from the terminal, as it seemed the least popular portion of the lot.

"If I didn't want to be noticed, I'd park out here in the hinterlands," Joe said as they cruised the rows of vehicles.

"Then what would you do?" Nick asked.

"Walk out to Congress Street and call a cab."

Nick nodded. "Then they wouldn't recall picking you up at the airport."

"I'll bet that's what Harwood did when he dumped his sister's car here."

Nick circled until they'd checked every vehicle in their area and met a patrol car searching the next section of the lot. They met the airport on-duty officer at the ticket booth once more.

"We haven't found any vehicles matching this license number," the patrolman reported. "There was a red Avalon in section C, but it had a different plate. We checked it on the computer, and it's legit. The owner came out of the terminal while we were running the plate, and she said she'd come to pick up her son and daughter-in-law. Everything checks out."

Nick turned to Joe. His blue eyes took on the same troubled gray hue as the waters of Casco Bay. "What now?"

Joe scowled as he looked back toward the terminal once more, thinking. Petra was in danger, and he had failed to stop it. He sent up a desperate prayer.

"Harwood didn't leave his stepsister's car here until twelve hours after he'd killed her," he said.

Nick nodded. "And it's only been a couple of hours since Petra got off work."

They walked toward Nick's car. Many thoughts collided in Joe's mind, but one came into focus. "Harwood drove out of Portland to dump Harriet Foster's body. Then he brought her car back here."

"Okay, but he killed her before he left town. I think we can assume Petra was alive when she got into the car with him."

Joe got into the passenger seat and buckled his seat belt. "Rex used to live above Augusta. He won't take Petra to the same place he took Harriet. He knows the police have found that site, and he'll stay away from there."

Nick started the engine. "You think he's headed to territory he knows well from his younger days?"

"Could be." Joe scratched his jaw. "Petra has friends in the neighborhood who know she was moving to Waterville this weekend. When I went to check her house tonight, a sweet old lady told me all about Petra's plans."

"The grapevine strikes again." Nick nodded. "Okay. So he may have known about her plans to move this weekend and stepped up his timetable on silencing her. We know he didn't wait for her at her house on Acton Street. He ambushed her when she left work. It's unlikely he'd take her back to her house or his, but I've got men keeping a watch on those places."

"Makes sense. But let's say he grabbed Petra and headed north. That seems the most likely scenario to me, given his history."

Nick turned toward the nearest on ramp for I-295. "But he might . . . Joe, I don't like to say this to you, but he might kill her, dump the body, and then take the car someplace else to divert the police."

It hurt to inhale, but Joe knew he had to face reality. "Right. But her car is the only lead we have right now. Let's go."

Nick winced and looked away.

"What?" Joe asked.

"It's getting late, and . . ."

"Oh, your shift is over, so you're quitting?"

"No, not at all. I'll stay on this with you. But we can't just take the car a hundred miles away. I'll have to ask for permission."

"We'll take my car."

Nick nodded. "Probably best. I'll call in and tell my sergeant I'm going to Augusta with you."

"Sidney," Joe corrected him.

"Sidney?"

"That's where Harwood grew up. Have the State Police on the lookout in Sidney. It's Harwood's home turf. I'm banking on a secluded road, off in the woods. Something off River Road or Pond Road in Sidney."

"I'll drop you where you left your car, and you pick me up at the station." Nick put the lights and siren on.

Petra drove northward by a winding course. They stopped in a small town, and Rex instructed her to pull in at a self-service gas station. When she put the transmission in park beside one of the gas pumps, he said, "Turn off the engine."

She did, wondering how he would work things. Was this her chance to summon help?

"Give me the key ring."

She hesitated, and the gun barrel grazed her neck again.

"Now."

She pulled the key from the ignition and held it up near her shoulder without looking at him. He snatched it.

"And your purse."

Petra's heart sank. She heard him rummaging through her things.

"Don't try anything," he said a moment later. "I'll have you covered every second."

He got out on the side near the gas pumps and slid a credit card into the self-pay slot. *Probably my card. He's too chintzy to bankroll his own crime.* The thought chilled her. Until now, she'd refused to think she might be minutes away from death, but she had to face it. There was only one reason Rex Harwood had kidnapped her at gunpoint. Harriet Foster's body had been found, and he saw Petra as the only link back to him. He didn't know Joe had already traced his extended family and confirmed that the dead woman was Rex's stepsister. And he didn't know Joe and Nick were fast digging up his motive.

She sneaked a look over the back of the seat. The contents of her purse were strewn across the backseat and on the floor. Her cell phone was nowhere to be seen. She hadn't thought to turn it on as she left the hospital. What if it was still in the side pocket of her leather bag?

Rex had the nozzle in the gas tank port and the numbers on the pump whirled. Forget the cell phone. If she opened the passenger door, could she hope to reach help? The only other customer pumping gas got in his car and drove away. Her heart sank. No one else was outside. The storefront was at least ten yards away. She had to try.

She unbuckled her seat belt stealthily and turned in the seat.

A tap on the glass of the passenger window startled her, and she jerked around toward the sound. Rex was leaning in against the side of the car staring at her. The muzzle of the pistol touched the glass eight inches from her temple.

Her chest constricted. She hadn't even moved over toward the other door. He wouldn't shoot her here in the open. Would he?

She glanced around. The paved area in front of the little store was still empty except for them. She supposed he could shoot, shove her over and drive off without anyone seeing a thing.

Rex's face clenched in a harsh glower. Maybe he was desperate enough to take a chance. For the first time, she looked past the gun barrel and noticed that he was wearing flesh-colored surgical gloves. She swallowed hard and turned around in the seat to face the steering wheel and buckled her belt.

Joe was glad he was driving. He just wished he had a light bar and a siren. Nick said nothing about his excessive speed, but spent the first half hour of their northward journey on the phone. As they approached a bridge undergoing repairs, traffic slowed to a crawl. Joe drummed his fingers on the steering wheel and imagined ways they could get through faster. Maybe if he leaned on the horn and Nick held his badge out the window . . . At last they pulled away from the construction zone.

"Take it easy, Joe."

"You want to drive?"

"No. You'd go bananas if I drove your car."

You got that right. "Harwood knows the area well. You got plenty of manpower out there?"

"They're arranging a road block on I-95 at the Augusta-Belgrade and Sidney exits," Nick said. "Everyone's watching for Petra's car. The Augusta, Waterville and Oakland P.D.s will help the State Police cover all the back roads in the Sidney area. And they sent an emergency bulletin to all the TV stations, but we don't know if any of them will broadcast it before the late news. I don't know what else we can do."

Joe glanced at his watch. "Another hour or so of daylight. Think, Nick!"

"What about?"

"The professor. When he killed Harriet Foster, he put her body in her car, drove it to Durham and dumped it. Then he drove the car back to Portland and put it in the airport lot the next morning."

"He must have left it somewhere overnight."

"Maybe. Unless he was driving around most of the night, looking for a good spot to leave the body. His wife was away, and she wouldn't have known when he came in."

"He could have waited until the busiest time in the morning, so the airport personnel would be less likely to remember him being there," Nick said.

"Maybe. And he could have left Harriet's car in a different parking lot while he went home for a few hours' sleep," Joe said. "A store parking lot or someplace like that. No one was looking for it then. But what's he going to do with Petra's car?"

Nick shrugged. "It could be anywhere right now except the airport."

"Right. What if he wants it to look like Petra's heading home? He might abandon her car in Waterville, near her sisters' house or their store, which is right beside my office."

"Okay. I'll ask Waterville P.D. to pay extra attention to those streets." Nick opened his phone.

When he was done with the call, Joe said, "Listen, if Harwood ditches the car, what will he do next?"

Nick hesitated. "I give up. What?"

"Exactly. When he left the airport in Portland, all he had to do was hail a cab. Or he could even have walked home, though it's quite a hike for a fifty-year-old man with a sedentary job."

"He does all that digging, though," Nick mused. "He can't be in too bad shape."

"Well, he's not in good enough shape to walk a hundred miles home from Sidney or Waterville."

"Aha. I follow you." Nick sat back and closed his eyes. "Public transportation, car rental, hitchhiking, stealing a car, or getting someone to pick him up."

"That about covers it." Joe frowned, ticking them off one by one in his brain. "I don't see him taking a bus, but we can have a patrolman check. The bus stop is out near the airport in Waterville. Two or three car dealers in town have rental businesses. I think that's a good bet. We should check Augusta, too. That's closer to home for him. But hitchhiking's too risky and too uncertain. If he thinks he can keep this from his wife, he's got to get back to Portland before midnight. He could explain that, but not an all-nighter."

"Joe."

"Hm?"

Joe looked over at Nick. His friend gritted his teeth. "Don't you think he's already contacted his wife to give her an excuse for why he's late coming home to dinner?"

"Possibly. Do we still have a patrol officer with Mrs. Harwood?"

Nick started punching buttons on his cell phone. "Wish I had my radio."

Joe stretched his back muscles and flexed his shoulders. Ten more minutes to Augusta. He decided to leave the interstate there and touch base with the officers at the road block.

The sun lowered behind them, casting long shadows on the road ahead. Nick's eyes were grim when he put away his phone.

"The detective squad is going nuts, but they're trying to cover all the bases in Portland. They haven't found anyone yet who saw Petra leave the hospital or knows where she parked today. The good news is, they took Mrs. Harwood to the station for questioning. She hasn't given them anything, but she asked for a lawyer, so they've stopped interviewing her. And so far as they know, Rex hasn't tried to contact her. He hasn't called his own house, and Mrs. H. wasn't carrying a cell phone."

"She's not in this," Joe said. "Harriet Foster's murder happened on the spur of the moment, while Mrs. Harwood was in Millinocket. I doubt very much her husband told her about it. In fact, I don't think she even knew he sold those antiques illegally. If she did, she wouldn't have been so friendly to me the other night."

He put on the turn signal, and they rolled down the Augusta-Belgrade exit. Cars were backed up around the curve of the ramp. Two police cars with flashing lights were parked where the ramp met Route 11.

"I'm getting out," Nick said. "Ease on through and pick me up down there, after I find out if they've got anything."

Joe hated inching down the exit one car length at a time. It was after eight o'clock, and he switched on his radio to catch the news headlines. "Police are looking for a Portland woman who is feared kidnapped this afternoon. Her car is a red Toyota Avalon, last year's model, license plate number . . ."

Joe pulled forward and a uniformed state trooper stepped to his car door. Joe nodded at him. "Hey, I'm Joe Tarleton, and I'm with Detective Wyatt over there." He pointed to where Nick was conversing with another officer.

The trooper called, "Is this gentleman with you?"

Nick nodded, said a few more words to the officer, and jogged to Joe's car. He plopped into the passenger seat and shut the door.

"Anything?" Joe asked.

"No. They're letting through most of the cars, but it still snarls up traffic. What do you think is our best bet?"

Joe pulled out onto the roadway. "Ernest Harwood had a country place in Sidney thirty or forty years ago. That's where Rex grew up. I think we should concentrate on that neighborhood."

"But we don't even know Rex came up here. He only took Harriet as far as Durham . . ."

"I know." Joe didn't like it one bit. "Nicky, we've got to do something. The way I figure, he knows they found Harriet's body and he's not going to chance dumping Petra so close to home. He'll go someplace where he knows he can hide a body better than he did the first one." The words were so crass that Joe felt a tremor of repulsion. It could be too late for Petra.

"Right," Nick said softly. "And Waterville P.D. has a patrol car on the street where your office is. They sent a detective to Petra's sisters' house to tell them what's going on and see if anything unusual has happened—if Petra's called them, for instance."

"Good." Joe wished again that Petra had leveled with her sisters. This was going to be rough for them. He drove in silence to the intersection where the road split between Belgrade and Sidney. Messalonskee Lake lay between the two towns.

"I'm sorry, Joe," Nick said. "We should have put her in protective custody."

"She wanted to finish out the work week." Joe shook his head in remorse. "I was stupid enough to let her do it." He sent up a silent prayer.

Chapter sixteen

Petra found it hard to breathe. She switched the car's lights on. It wasn't quite dusk yet, but she felt the end of their journey was near and she needed to do anything that would make her more visible and easier to find. Driving at gunpoint down a dirt road in Sidney didn't boost her hopes.

"Slow down."

Her heart hammered and her hands shook as she guided the car along the isolated road. Were they headed for Great Sidney Bog? *He could throw a hundred bodies in there and they wouldn't be found for years.*

"There! Pull in there."

She braked and looked where he gestured. An even smaller road led off between the birches and poplars. A woods road, more like a jeep trail.

She nosed the car in under the branches and braked.

"A little farther." His voice was quiet, near her right ear.

She shivered and obeyed.

"All right. Put it in Park." She hesitated, wondering what would happen if she threw it in reverse and floored it. The hard metal of the pistol muzzle pressing against the back of her head answered the question. "Do it now."

Her joints turned to rubber as she did what he demanded. He opened the rear door. A cool breeze wafted through the car.

"Get out," he said.

She groped for the door handle and pulled it with numbed fingers. When she swung her legs out and looked up at him, he stood impassively watching her with the gun in his right hand and a coil of manila rope in his left. Her mouth went dry.

"Come along, Petra."

"Where are we going?" She hated the quiver in her voice.

"You'll see."

"We can't drive?"

"Just leave the car here. I'll need it later."

"But . . ."

He sighed. "Let's not be tiresome. The police will find your car safe in your garage when they look there. Right where you parked when you got home from work this evening."

She said nothing but eyed him cautiously. If Joe were here, what would he do? She felt that she ought to memorize every detail—Rex's clothes, the gloves, the pistol, the rope—just as she'd tried to commit to memory the turns they'd made after they reached a point she recognized in Sidney. But for what? She would never have a chance to tell anyone. She disappeared from Portland, but her car would be found there after Rex returned it to her garage. It would be easy for him, although she'd changed the locks on the house. He had her garage door opener now. Would Joe know somehow that her car had been driven an extra two hundred miles tonight? Not likely. What could she do to get out of this?

"Give me the keys," Rex said.

She pulled them from the ignition and stood, her knees shaking, and dropped the key ring into his hand without touching him.

"Turn around," Rex said. "Follow the path."

She walked with wooden legs through the trees. A phoebe sang, and a gray squirrel ran across the trail not two yards in front of her. It wasn't fair. She ought to be able to do something.

"You could have avoided this, you know," he said behind her. "If you'd only kept quiet."

She said nothing but kept walking slowly. Ahead, she saw a glimmer of light on water.

"That's it," Rex said quietly. "Go right up to the bank. It's a pretty spot. I always loved it here."

Petra's lungs felt as though they would explode with each breath. If she'd wanted to scream, she wouldn't have been able to. She stepped slowly toward the water. The trail petered out, and the legs of her light blue uniform pants brushed the long grass aside as she approached the rim of the pond. Trees grew within a few feet of the brink, and several boulders dotted the shore.

"Closer to the edge," Rex said. "This was my favorite fishing spot."

Her mind raced. If he shot her on the edge of the pond, she would fall in. What was the rope for?

"Stop now."

She looked over her shoulder, and she knew. He was kicking at a rock about the size of a football. Heavy enough to weight her body to the bottom of the pond?

She pulled in a breath, her mind racing. Could she somehow overbalance him and push him over the brink instead? Heroines in movies did it. But she doubted Rex would get carelessly close to the edge. How deep was the water? He must know and be confident it would conceal her for a long time. If she were wounded, how long could she hold her breath? And if he tied the rock to her body, how would she get free of it?

He dropped the rope next to the rock and faced her.

"Now then, don't you want to turn around? Look out over the pond. It's truly beautiful."

She started to turn, helpless to do anything else.

A sudden movement from behind a large rock startled her. A man stood up with a fishing rod in one hand. He wore jeans and a Colby College T-shirt. His dark hair gleamed in the last rays of sunlight, and he smiled from behind wire-rimmed glasses.

"Hello, folks. Come to enjoy the view?"

She could tell the instant his gaze focused on Rex's hands. His jaw dropped and his eyes widened.

Petra sucked in a huge breath and ran toward the pond. In two steps, she was at the berm. She launched her body downward, keeping low, and extended her hands before her. As her face cut the water, she heard an explosion behind her.

She pushed hard with her legs, angling down and away from the shore, to her left. On her third kick, her hands struck bottom. She leveled off, took two strokes with her arms, and headed for the surface. As soon as she broke through, she grabbed another breath and dove again. She and her sisters had practiced surface dives together—sticking their feet up like a mermaid's tail. This time she tried to keep them beneath the water. *No splash.* She hadn't heard another gunshot. What did that mean? She swam on and on, her lungs burning. At last she surfaced and looked back. She couldn't see anyone on shore in the shadowy twilight. Wasn't that the spot where she'd dived?

She turned and struck out for the far side of the pond. A hundred yards or so. She could make it. As she swam she tried to orient herself. The car . . . the road . . . If she climbed out of the pond near that leaning pine tree and walked east, away from the sunset, she ought to strike the dirt road soon.

Her feet kicked bottom, and she stood. Her hair and her loose cotton uniform hugged her body, dripping. She slogged through the shallows. The bank wasn't as steep on this side, and she thought she could climb out. The water beneath the pine was murky, and she shivered. The first thing she would do when she reached safety was to check for leeches. She grabbed a sticky branch and pulled herself up out of the water. Her shoes sloshed and squeaked.

As she shoved back her sopping hair, something struck the trunk of the pine near her cheek, and a *pow* echoed over the water. She ducked and scrambled beneath the leaning bole of the tree and into the dark woods beyond.

Joe drove slowly, scanning the roadside. "You sure this is it?" he asked.

Nick nodded. "They had the town clerk look it up. This is where his family lived."

Joe signaled for a driveway and drove up before a white clapboard house. "Her car's not here."

"Not where we can see it." Nick got out of the car and bounded up the steps. Joe followed, peering about the yard in the half light. A stocky young man opened the door to Nick's peremptory knock.

Nick held up his badge. "I'm police detective Nick Wyatt. We're looking for a man who used to live here. Rex Harwood. Has he been here?"

The man blinked at him. "I don't think so. What's he look like?"

"Tall, thin, dark hair with some gray, dark eyes, glasses, age fifty."

The man shook his head. "Nobody like that's been around here lately."

"So you didn't know the Harwood family?"

"No, can't say as I did. When did they live here?"

"A long time ago. Thirty or forty years."

The man laughed. "That's older than me."

Joe stepped forward. "Have you seen a red car around here today? A Toyota Avalon."

The man shook his head. "Nope. You wanna come in? My wife might have seen someone."

Nick started to follow him inside when his phone rang.

"Wyatt. Yeah? Hold on." He looked at Joe. "Are we near the Quaker Road?"

The homeowner stepped onto the porch. "You can cut across right down there at the corner." He pointed down the road.

"Great," Nick said. "They found Petra's car in the woods over there."

Petra moved with as much caution as she could at first. She considered holing up behind some undergrowth, but the sound of tramping footsteps and breaking branches soon pushed her into a run. She trudged through the forest, losing her bearings after a few yards. She could no longer tell where the sun had gone down. Walking in a straight line would be better than no plan. She sighted ahead, from one tree to another. The white bark of the birches let her see them several yards away. Soon it would be too dark even for that.

Hurrying along, she caught her toe on a root and sprawled on the ground. Her knee hurt. She hauled herself up and limped onward. Beneath a large hardwood she paused, listening. At first she heard nothing but the stirring branches above her, but soon the unmistakable sounds of pursuit reached her. She looked up, considering climbing the tree, but the lowest branches were too high for her. *If he spotted me in a tree, he could shoot me, and I wouldn't have a chance.*

She stumbled on, but her wrenched knee definitely slowed her down. She leaned against a large, moss-covered rock and gasped for breath, shivering.

A shot rang out, closer than she'd bargained for. She threw herself on the ground behind the rock. As she lay still, she heard quick hoofbeats retreating.

He must have seen a deer and thought it was me. Thank you, Lord. She hoped the deer escaped.

From a short distance away, she heard him trampling brush and thrashing about. The noise grew fainter, and she waited. At last she couldn't hear him anymore, but she continued to lie still. The wind picked up, and the rustling of the trees increased, blotting out the sounds she strained to hear.

After another ten minutes, she rolled cautiously to her back and stared up between dancing leaves. She could barely see a sprinkling of stars. Could she find her way back to the clearing where the pond was? If so, she thought she could make her way to her car. But maybe Rex would wait there for her. She stood up. Her clammy wet clothes clung to her skin. She set out slowly, one hand extended before her so she wouldn't crash into a tree. A faint wail reached her and she stopped. Above her pounding pulse and the sighing wind, she caught it again: a distant siren. She adjusted her path toward where the road must be.

Joe stood on the gas pedal in order to keep up with the police car ahead of him. He wished the officer would kill that annoying siren. It was giving him a headache, not to mention alerting every criminal in the county of their presence. They veered around a curve.

Nick grabbed the armrest. "I bet that's the dirt road they were talking about right there."

The police car shot past the road Nick had indicated, but Joe slowed and turned in. The town clerk had relayed a message that the Harwoods owned a wood lot in this area, and Rex Harwood was the owner of record, having paid the taxes since his father's death. A quarter of a mile farther down the road, Joe spotted two more squad cars and an ambulance parked to one side. He parked on the shoulder and jumped out, heading straight for the EMTs.

"What've you got?" Joe barked.

"Forty-year-old male, gunshot wound to the abdomen."

197

Joe glanced at the man's taut face. "He tell you anything?"

"Yeah, the police arrived first, and they interviewed him."

Joe hurried to join Nick. Darkness was falling fast. Nick was with two officers just inside the verge of the woods, examining a car with their flashlights. Petra's car.

"So what did the wounded man tell you?" Nick asked the state trooper who seemed to be in charge.

"He said he was fishing and two people came along. The woman jumped in the water, and the man shot him," said the state trooper.

Nick introduced Joe and asked if the officers had found anything important at the car.

"Not really. It's locked. Nobody inside, but it looks like there's a purse in the back seat."

A man in plain clothes knelt at the back bumper, his arm underneath the back of the car.

"Got it." He pulled out a hide-a-key case and handed it to the trooper. While he stood and brushed off the knees of his pants, the trooper extracted the car key. Joe didn't think he could stand another moment of the images assaulting his brain.

"Open the trunk first," he said.

The trooper shrugged and tried the key in the trunk lock. The lid swung up, and they all looked inside. Like Petra's house, her car trunk was neat. Spare tire, wool blanket, jack, an emergency flare box, and a folding shovel.

"Where's the fishing hole?" Joe asked.

The trooper pointed down the overgrown woods road. "We've got two officers in by the pond."

The police car Joe had followed came down the road, slower this time, and pulled to a stop. The driver cut the siren and got out.

Joe wasn't in the mood to wait while the State Police and the local cops scrimmaged over whose turf they were on. He pushed aside the branches that nearly touched the hood of the car and struck off down the path.

"Sir," the trooper called. "You can't enter the crime scene, sir."

Joe ignored him and kept walking. He heard someone running to catch up with him.

"Joe, they'll organize a search," Nick said.

"No time."

"You'll compromise the scene."

Joe whirled on him. "Petra's in trouble. She may be dead. You can't keep me away from that pond."

They walked onward. Nick looked at him once and said, "Joe—"

"What?"

Nick sighed and shook his head.

They broke out of the dark woods into a clearing mostly filled with a serene pond about two hundred yards wide. A stream trickled out of it toward the highway. *Good fishing spot.* Two uniformed officers were searching through the tall grass near the edge of the water with flashlights.

Nick touched his arm. "Stay here. You don't want to make them mad. Let me talk to them."

Joe ran a hand through his hair and nodded. He respected the protocol of the crime scene. Nick left him and approached the officers. In the distance, a siren began and then faded. The ambulance, Joe thought. He hoped the fisherman made it.

He looked around. Something lay on the ground a few yards away, and he eased toward it.

Nick came back to him.

"They found a lot of jumbled footprints and the man's fishing gear. No sign of Petra or Harwood."

Joe nodded toward the ground. "What about this?"

"Yeah, they saw that rope lying there beside the rock. Don't know if Harwood brought it or what. It could have been there a while."

"What now?"

"The trooper out by her car is organizing a search. If we don't find her by morning, they'll ask for divers to check the pond."

Joe felt as if his heart stopped beating for a few seconds. He sucked in a breath. "Okay."

Nick laid a hand on his shoulder. "The fisherman said Petra—that is, the woman—dived into the water. Then Harwood shot him. He doesn't know what happened to the two of them after that. He crawled over to his knapsack, got out his cell phone, and called 911."

"What did he say about the woman?"

"She was pretty, and she was wearing a light blue outfit. He thought it was a uniform."

"That's what she wears to work." Joe looked out over the dark water. He couldn't bear to think her body might lie beneath the surface while they stood here talking. "What can we do?"

"Let's go back to the cars. They're going to keep patrolling along the roads that bound this stretch of woods."

"It's a big patch."

"So I'm told. Come on." Nick touched his arm and steered him back toward the path.

When they reached Petra's car, Joe saw that several more vehicles had arrived and a knot of people clustered around the trooper.

". . . we'll patrol these roads continuously," the officer said. "The canine unit should be here soon. The suspect is armed, and he didn't hesitate to shoot a witness. We don't want anyone else hurt. I don't want anyone going in the woods except law enforcement personnel wearing body armor."

Joe noted that a reporter was already on the scene, scribbling in a notebook. Another cruiser approached with its lights flashing. The blinding blue strobe drew his eyes. That made five police cars and counting.

The car was a couple of hundred yards away when a figure stumbled out of the woods onto the gravel road in the path of the cruiser.

The police car swerved and ground to a halt. Petra stopped her frantic run and gasped for breath, fearing her knees would buckle. An officer leaped from the car and grabbed her upper arms.

"Are you all right, ma'am?"

"Yes. No. A man tried to kill me." She panted and bent over, hugging her aching side.

"Petra, it's me."

She whirled at the familiar voice and focused on the man running toward her out of the shadows.

"Joe!"

She threw herself into his arms.

He held her as the policemen and volunteers gathered around, staring. She was dripping wet, but that didn't stop him.

"It's all right," he said. "You're safe."

Nick stepped up behind her and draped his jacket over her shoulders. Petra sobbed and Joe wrapped one arm over the jacket and pulled her closer. He pushed her wet hair aside and whispered in her ear, "Thank you, Lord. Thank you for bringing Petra back to me." Then he looked deep in her eyes. "Come on. We'll get you warm." He kissed her temple, and she clung to him.

An hour later, Petra lay on a gurney in the exam room waiting for the doctor to return.

"This is silly," she said. "I'm not hurt. Just my knee, and that feels a lot better since they gave me the ibuprofen."

"Just let the doc look you over," Joe murmured. He lifted her hand to his lips and kissed her fingers. "You're still cold." He pulled the blanket up to her chin.

"I thought I'd freeze after I got out of the water," she admitted. "It turned really cold tonight."

"And you're probably in shock, too."

The nurse who had attended her earlier poked her head in the doorway. "Miss Wilson, your sisters are in the waiting room. Would you like them to wait there, or to come in here?"

"Well . . . how long is the doctor going to be?"

"Let them come in," Joe growled, and she stared at him in surprise.

The nurse went out.

"What's wrong, Joe?" Petra slid her fingers through his dark hair.

He leaned into her touch. "Nothing. That is, nothing except I almost lost you tonight, and it was my own stupid fault."

"No, it wasn't. Don't say that."

"I feel like it was. And I hadn't even gotten around to asking you if you like baseball."

She frowned at that in momentary confusion. "Red Sox, but . . ."

"Fantastic."

"Joe, you helped collect the evidence. And if you hadn't done all that background work on Rex, no one would have known about his family's property in Sidney. The police wouldn't have been looking for me up here."

"That's beside the point. If Nick and I had acted earlier, you might not have been in this fix at all." He glanced toward the doorway. "You need to let your sisters fuss over you. You go and almost get killed, and they don't even know what's going on. You need to let them in, Petra. Let them love you."

She looked into his eyes, knowing he was right. "I will. Thank you."

He leaned over to kiss her.

202

"Well, excuse us," Keilah said from the doorway. "We heard our sister was in here having a crisis."

"You heard wrong, kiddo," Joe said. "They probably said getting kisses."

Petra smiled. "This is ridiculous. I'm not hurt. I didn't even get any leeches."

"Leeches?" Bethany pushed past Keilah and came to stand by the stretcher. "Petra, what is going on?"

"The police said you were kidnapped," Keilah added. "Scared us to death."

Petra sighed. "Sit down, girls. I have a story to tell you. And if the doctor hasn't checked in by the time I'm done telling it, I'm leaving anyway. I want to go home and sleep in my tower room and snuggle up to my dog."

"Well, hey," said a deep voice. She looked up and saw Nick Wyatt lounging against the door frame.

"Hello, Nick," Petra said.

"Nicky, my man." Joe stood up. "What's the word?"

"We got Harwood. He was crashing around in the woods not far from where Petra came out onto the road. If that fisherman hadn't been able to call us . . . Well, let's not think about that. The doctor says he's going to make it."

"Oh, I'm so glad," Petra said.

Nick walked to the gurney and smiled at her. "You don't look so bad now that you've dried off."

"Thank you, I think." She reached to squeeze the hand he extended.

"Joe, can I speak to you outside for a minute?" Nick asked.

"Sure." He looked at Petra. "Don't go away. I'll be back."

"Don't worry," said Keilah, appropriating Joe's chair. "We won't let her go anywhere. She's going to tell us every miserable detail." As the two men left the room, she turned to Petra. "Who is that gorgeous man?"

Petra smiled, feeling suddenly very tired. "Joe's friend. He's married."

Keilah pouted. "Too bad. Okay, spill it."

"Yes, and start at the beginning." Bethany walked around the gurney and sat on the windowsill on the other side.

Petra lay back against the pillows and looked up at the tiled ceiling. "It all started the night I witnessed a murder."

Epilogue

Petra worked feverishly at the kitchen counter one afternoon a week later, when Keilah and Bethany came home from the shop. She had a vase filled with deep red roses and a canning jar overflowing with pink ones.

"Hey, have you guys got another vase?" she asked.

Keilah stared at the white roses still in their box lined with green tissue paper. "What on earth? Are you starting a florist shop?"

Petra laughed. "No, they're all from Joe."

Bethany laid her purse on the kitchen island. "I think there's one in the pantry." She came back a moment later with a large jardinière.

Petra's phone rang, and she grabbed it from the counter.

"Joe! Hey!"

Keilah grinned and whispered, "Go talk to him. We'll fix these for you."

Petra walked through to the airy living room as Joe asked, "How you doing?"

She chuckled. "I'm doing great. Overrun with roses."

"Oh." He paused. "Do you like them?"

"They're beautiful. Thank you."

"You're welcome. I hope it wasn't too . . ."

She listened carefully, trying to catch his mood. "I did wonder why there were three bouquets."

"Well, see, I got to the florist shop and they had all these flowers. I didn't know what to choose. The lady started telling me that all the colors of roses have different meanings. So I picked three that I thought might . . . express your feelings. I hope you'll pick the ones you like best for our date tonight."

Petra frowned. "I like them all. What did she say they mean?"

"Tell you what, why don't you wear a white one tonight if you just want to be friends, now that your case is closed and we don't have to work together any more."

She didn't like the sound of that, but Joe rushed on.

"Or a pink one if you want to keep dating for a while and sort of keep what we have now. I mean . . . I think we have something pretty good, but . . . The red ones are for . . . for if you're ready to think about it."

"Think about what?" she asked, baffled.

"Well, if you want to get married."

She caught her breath. If this was a proposal, it was the strangest one she'd ever heard of. But she found her pulse throbbing in anticipation. "Okay . . . I'll see you later, Joe." She hung up and walked back to the kitchen, still smiling.

"What's so funny?" Bethany asked. She and Keilah had combined the three colors of roses into one huge bouquet.

"That looks great," Petra said. "I'm just laughing at Joe. He's so sweet and funny." She told them the mysteries of the floral language.

Bethany smiled and swept the clippings from the counter into the trash can. "I think he's one of the nicest men I've ever met. But I wonder what yellow roses mean."

Keilah laughed. "That florist really sold him. If she'd kept on with her spiel, I bet she could have talked Joe into two or three dozen more."

"Oh, stop it." Petra put her hand out to touch one of the delicate blooms and bent to sniff them. She sighed.

"We could make you a corsage with all three," Bethany suggested.

"Oh, I don't think there's any need for that," Petra assured her.

Joe arrived on the dot of seven, and Keilah let him in.

"Petra will be right down, Joe." She led him into the living room, and Joe stopped short. The flowers he'd sent were all in a big ceramic jug on a table between the windows.

Keilah nodded at them. "Impressive, I must say."

"Uh, thanks." Joe gulped. Maybe he'd overdone it a bit. Would Petra feel he was pushing her? He wished he could go back a few hours and forget about, uh, floral communication.

"So what did you and Nick find out about the Toby jugs?" Keilah asked.

Joe turned to her in relief. This he could handle. "Well, we knew Harriet Foster's mother left the Toby jug collection to Harriet in her will. Her brother told the police that when Harriet came for the funeral, Rex told her he would have it packed up and shipped to her. Instead, Rex sold it and kept the money. He kept giving her excuses. After waiting nearly four years and getting nothing, Harriet drove to Portland to confront Rex about it."

"That's what Petra saw."

"That's what I figure," Joe agreed. "She grabbed the one remaining piece from the collection and threatened to go to the police."

Keilah wrinkled her nose. "He kept the best Toby jug for himself, and when she touched it, he panicked and strangled her."

"Yup. If Petra hadn't seen it and called the cops, he'd have gotten away with it."

Keilah nodded. "I'm so proud of her. Excuse me, Joe. Beth and I are working on the books. Yell if you need anything." She squeezed his arm and disappeared through the hall door.

Joe shoved his hands into his pockets and walked over to get a closer look at the flowers. That was a lot of roses. Their fragrance filled the air.

Have I still got a chance with her? Maybe this was stupid.

He turned away. No doubt Petra would wear a white rose tonight and put him out of his misery. Maybe he'd dressed up for nothing. He flipped up the end of his new necktie and eyed it critically. He probably could have worn an old one and she wouldn't have noticed.

He spun back toward the vase and tried to count the white blossoms. Twelve. No, thirteen. That couldn't be right. He tried counting the pink, but his nerves made him keep glancing toward the doorway and he couldn't keep track. Well, there were eleven or twelve red, he was sure of that much. What if the florist hadn't counted right?

A swish that only a woman's skirt could make came from the doorway, and he whipped around. She'd caught him.

"Hello, Joe. They are fabulous, aren't they?"

Petra smiled so brilliantly that it took him a moment to register the rose she held in her hands. She walked slowly toward him, the deep red of the bloom contrasted against her filmy white dress. He couldn't speak, much as he wanted to.

She stopped a foot from him and twirled the stem, looking down at the flower. Then she raised her gaze to meet his.

"I like this one," she whispered.

He pulled her to him, then jerked away, realizing he would crush the rose between them. Probably that thing had thorns. She smiled and held it out carefully as she wrapped her arms around him, holding the stem behind him as she settled into his embrace. He looked down into her eyes. He couldn't think of anything clever to say, so he went with the obvious.

"Petra, I love you."

She raised her lips to meet his.

"I love you, too."

Perfect.

The End

About the Author

Susan Page Davis is a native of central Maine. She and her husband, Jim, have six children and ten grandchildren. She now lives in western Kentucky. She's the author of more than eighty mystery, romantic suspense, and historical romance novels and is the winner of the Carol Award, two Faith Hope & Love Chapter RWA's Readers' Choice Awards, and two Will Rogers Medallions for Excellence in Western Fiction. Visit her website at: https://susanpagedavis.com.

Dear Reader,

Writing Petra and Joe's story was a real challenge for me. It deals with searching for truth and standing firm when others believe you are wrong. Petra's journey from guilt and isolation to forgiveness and fellowship coincides with the solving of a heinous crime. Getting to know my characters is always a spiritual journey for me, too, as I walk with them through their problems and resolution.

I belong to a very special group—I'm one of four sisters. The other three are women I know I can turn to in time of need. They will always love me without being judgmental. They put up with my foibles, though they may tease a little. And they can always make me laugh. Sisters are a very special gift from God. Petra reclaimed her place among the Wilson sisters in this story. If you don't have sisters, I urge you to find godly women you feel comfortable with and form a special bond with them as sisters in Christ.

I love hearing from my readers. You can visit me at my Web site at: https://susanpagedavis.com.

Find me on Facebook at: https://www.facebook.com/susanpagedavisauthor.

Susan Page Davis

Discussion Questions

1. Petra witnesses a horrible crime in chapter one and calls the police. Have you ever seen someone commit a crime, or an act that you knew was wrong though not illegal, and struggled with what to do?

2. When the police find no evidence and dismiss her claims, Petra feels abandoned and helpless. What would you do if you knew something important, but no one believed you?

3. During this time of crisis, Petra returns to prayer and begins to sort through her broken relationship with God. Why do difficult times bring us to spiritual introspection? What can we do at those times to make sure the resolutions we form in crisis are carried out when the pressure is off?

4. In chapter two, Joe has a very bad day. It's so bad, he doesn't feel like praying or listening to God. Have you ever felt that way? What should Joe do, and what do you do in times like this?

5. How did Joe's annoying new neighbors turn out to be a blessing in his life? How was he a blessing to the sisters?

6. Petra gives several reasons for not telling her sisters about the murder. She doesn't want to worry them. She's afraid they won't believe her. Near the end, she realizes part of her hesitation is pride. Has pride kept you from being open and honest with people you love? How can you remedy that?

7. Petra's dog, Mason, brings her great joy, but he's also caused her some headaches. Do you have a special pet? What does he bring to your life? What types of responsibility do pets bring?

8. As a woman living alone, Petra takes safety precautions. How do you balance relying on God for safety with common sense measures? Has your need for safety ever kept you from doing something you wanted to do?

9. What Petra did was not always as important as what Rex thought she did. Petra and Rex's gossiping neighbors also played a role in bringing the story to a violent end. How can misperceptions and rumors endanger people?

10. Our society puts a high value on "unconditional love." Yet even Joe has a moment when he feels he must test Petra's claims before he goes on with the investigation. Is there a time when others must earn our respect or love? What danger is there in trusting or loving a person without knowing all his underlying motives and conflicts?

11. Joe is careful not to lie to Mrs. Harwood and others he talks to in his investigation. How does this hamper his work? Would it be wrong for him to tell people he is a policeman, archaeologist, or other professional? Is it wrong when he lets people think he is a policeman? On the job, he takes pictures of people without their knowing about it in order to prove their crimes. Is this wrong?

12. Petra carries her guilt for her role in Danny's death for many years. How did this shape her interactions with other people and with God? What scripture could you give her to encourage her to leave the guilt behind?

Some of Susan Page Davis's Other Books
(See all her titles at https://susanpagedavis.com)

Maine Justice Series
    The Priority Unit
    Fort Point
    Found Art
    Heartbreaker Hero
    The House Next Door
    The Labor Day Challenge
    Ransom of the Heart
Just Cause
Hearts in the Crosshairs
Frasier Island Series
    Frasier Island
    Finding Marie
    Inside Story
Breaking News
The Saboteur
The Charm Bracelet
Mainely Mysteries Series
Trail to Justice
The Crimson Cipher
The Island Bride
Prairie Dreams Series
    The Lady's Maid
    Lady Anne's Quest
    A Lady in the Making
The Ladies' Shooting Club Series
    The Sheriff's Surrender
    The Gunsmith's Gallantry
    The Blacksmith's Bravery
Echo Canyon
The Outlaw Takes a Bride
Captive Trail

Cowgirl Trail
Alaska Weddings
Maine Brides
    The Prisoner's Wife
    The Castaway's Bride
    The Lumberjack's Lady
Wyoming Brides
    Protecting Amy
    The Oregon Escort
    Wyoming Hoofbeats
White Mountain Brides
    Return to Love
    A New Joy
    Abiding Peace
Almost Arizona
River Rest
My Heart Belongs in the Superstition Mountains
The Seafaring Women of the Vera B.
Love Comes to the Castle
Revolution at Barncastle Inn
Mrs. Mayberry Meets Her Match
The Reliable Cowboy

CPSIA information can be obtained
at www.ICGtesting.com
Printed in the USA
LVHW041642010519
616262LV00004B/584/P